The HEARTland—that place between the coasts where real people live. They work and play, laugh and cry, meet and fall in love. If they stumble and fall, they pick themselves up again and continue to fight the good fight. God and family always come first, friends a close second.

You know these people. They are always in the middle of things, the heart and soul of their families and communities. They will give their all for those they love. Their beliefs are unshakable.

In my second HEARTland ROMANCE, ***THE RIGHT KEY***, Karen McGraw and Gregg Watson continue to struggle with their attraction for one another. She's the worse possible choice for him, and he for her. Karen explains to Lori in *DREAMS RESTORED*, *"As far as Gregg Watson is concerned, there is no neutral ground between cops and reporters. It's all out war and take no prisoners!"*

Gregg is burned out as a cop. The twins are in college now and he's ready to retire to his ranch, but he has one last case to solve—one that requires Karen's help. As they work together, Karen sees a side of Gregg she never suspected and he realizes that all his preconceived notions about her have been way off base …

My third HEARTland ROMANCE will be available in the near future at www.lulu.com. You will meet Kris and learn about Matt in ***THE RIGHT KEY.*** Look for their story, ***PROMISES KEPT,*** coming soon.

I hope you enjoy these characters as much as I have enjoyed creating them. I wish you FAITH, HOPE & LOVE. May God Bless.

Eva O'Connor

HEARTland Series Book 2:

THE RIGHT KEY

by

Eva O'Connor

Lulu.com

HEARTland Series Book 2: THE RIGHT KEY
by Eva O'Connor

ISBN: 978-0-6151-8026-7

Cover Photograph by the author

Fix your thoughts on what is true and good and right. Think about things that are pure and lovely, and dwell on the fine, good things in others. Philippians 4:8 TLB

To Judy who inspired us all.

And to Travis, Alan, Ross, Wanda,
Barbara B, Barbara M, Tom, Neva
and all the other wonderful writers
in the San Angelo Writers' Club.
Without your support I would never
have had the courage to let my
writing see the light of day.

And to Doug, always.
Thanks for being there.

CHAPTER ONE

God, I could sure use some help on this case about now. Police officer Gregg Watson threw out the casual reminder as he neared the curve where he had found the two bodies in a burning car a week ago. Newly erected white crosses beckoned in the hope they would attract the attention of someone with information on the as yet unidentified victims.

Gregg touched the brakes lightly as he eased into the exit leading to the roadside park. His long, grueling week had ended and he wanted to check the crosses one last time before driving back to his ranch for the weekend.

He looked ahead, squinting against the sun, and then braked harder. A car was parked near the entrance, and someone knelt beside the two simple markers. Gregg frowned, suddenly torn. As much as he wanted to know the identity of the victims, he dreaded facing a family member with news of their loved one's death.

He brought his truck to a stop and got out, closing the door as quietly as possible. The woman stood now, a hand to her face. He hesitated, unsure whether or not to approach her. She raised her head and looked at him.

Gregg felt the breath leave his lungs. "Karen?" His voice expressed both uncertainty and concern. "What—I mean, do you know these kids?"

Karen McGraw raised a hand to brush at the tears on her face. The gesture bought time as she stared at Gregg Watson.

How could she possibly explain to this hard-bitten policeman how the sight of the crosses had affected her?

Everyone knew what those white crosses meant. Two people had lost their lives on this curve, and it must have happened recently, since the last time she'd passed this way. Her reporter's instinct, and curiosity, had led her to stop. She knew from past experience that Gregg didn't appreciate either of those qualities in her.

He looked different today, she noted irrelevantly, then realized that she had never before seen him out of uniform. Today he stood tall and rugged in plaid shirt and faded jeans. Her mouth twisted. Too bad he looked every bit as good as he did in his uniform. And too bad, still, that he made her feel just as inadequate, just as uncertain.

Karen shook her head. "I don't know," she said, answering his question. "Who are they?"

She saw his expression harden. "I might have known. Just after a story, as usual." He kicked at a fallen branch with the toe of his boot.

She put out her hand in an unconsciously pleading gesture. "Don't start, please, Gregg!" Her voice came out low and husky with the tears that still threatened. "I stopped to see if I might know them. I've been away for a couple of weeks, and the crosses weren't here when I left. I wondered what happened. I—who are they?" she asked a second time.

Gregg studied her as if he'd never seen her before. After a moment, he pulled himself back and focused on her again. "I don't know," he said, running a hand through his dark hair.

"You don't know?" Karen repeated. "Who put up the crosses?"

"I did."

She stared at him. "Why?"

"I hoped somehow they might lead me to the family—or families—of these kids. I've spent all week trying to find some clue—"

"Didn't they have identification? Something—anything—"

He threw her a glance. "I may not be a reporter of your caliber, but give me some credit."

"What about photos, drawings?" she asked. "Couldn't you—?"

"It's not that simple, Karen." Something in his voice brought her eyes to his face. Carefully impassive, it revealed nothing, but she knew he wasn't telling her everything.

She looked around the glade. A huge tree stood a few feet from the crosses. A tree that now had a ghastly blackened scar along the trunk. She glanced up. Singed, shriveled leaves drifted down on the breeze. At her feet she saw tender green grass peeking up through a scorched mat covering an area about twenty feet in diameter. A faint smell had been teasing her and she now identified it as burned vegetation. Her stomach twisted and her knees threatened to buckle.

Gregg caught her arm. "Sit down." He led her over to a bench, then propped a booted foot on the smooth stone and leaned over her, an elbow on his knee.

"You're much too good at your job." For the first time in all their stormy encounters, she detected admiration in his voice, reluctant thought it may be.

Karen looked at him. "You found them?"

He straightened and turned away. "Yes."

"I'm sorry."

He shrugged. "One of the less pleasant aspects of my job."

"Do you want to talk about it?" Karen offered.

He looked down at her. "And read about it in tomorrow's paper? I don't think so!"

She stared at him. "I wouldn't do that! Gregg, you can't believe I operate that way!"

His gaze shifted and he made no reply.

"You can't have that low an opinion of my profession." She swallowed, more hurt than she wanted to admit. "Or maybe it isn't my profession we're talking about here."

Gregg shoved his hands in his pockets, but still did not answer her.

Karen sighed. His closed expression and the coldness in his eyes pierced her soul. She felt tears threaten again. "What did I ever do to deserve such low regard from you?"

For a moment she thought he would not speak, then he shrugged. "People with my job have to tell families like these what happened to their children. People with your job then shove a microphone in their face and ask them how they feel to learn their child is dead. I can do without your shock tactics—"

"That's not the way I work!" Karen defended. She had risen to her feet, but now she sank back to the bench, her expression defeated. "What's the use? You've disliked me from the beginning. I don't know why it matters anymore."

Dear Father, please give me an opportunity to show Gregg the real me. That I'm nothing like he thinks I am.

Gregg watched her, almost convinced the tears sparkling in her dark eyes were real. "Would you like a chance to change your image?"

Not exactly what he had in mind, but he had prayed for help.

She looked up. "My image?"

"Well—my opinion of you, then."

"How?"

"Help me with this case."

"I beg your pardon?"

"I need to identify these kids. It's no longer just professional. It's become personal for me. I've spent over a week and gotten no where. I'll bet you know angles I wouldn't even consider. You have sources and resources. Trust me, the byline will be all yours. I just want to know who they are, so I can tell their families."

"Aren't you afraid I'll shove a microphone in their faces?" Bitterness twisted her face and tinged her voice.

He shook his head. "Not this time. Not after what you'll go through if you decide to help me."

Karen searched his face, her gaze uncertain. She stood up and turned away, arms folded across her chest.

Gregg studied her as he waited for an answer. The rays of the setting sun filtered through the trees, setting off red and gold highlights in the warm brown hair tumbling around her shoulders. He'd never seen her dressed casually before, in slacks and a cotton shirt, open at the throat. When working she wore skirts that displayed more of her long legs than he felt comfortable in seeing. He found himself wondering if he might be less hostile toward her had she not been so attractive. He half suspected his reaction was defensive. Something about her put his every instinct for self-preservation on the alert.

Karen raised her head and turned back to face him. "I'll do it. Not to change your opinion of me—that'll have to happen on its own—but because there's a story here that needs to be told. Shall I come by your office on Monday?"

"Make it Tuesday," he said. "I'm taking a day off."

She raised her brows. "How nice for you!"

His gaze hardened. "Since I haven't had a day off in two weeks, I think the taxpayers can afford it."

Karen's glance fell. He always ended up making her look small. She shrugged, a gesture that didn't quite come off, and felt her lips tremble.

"I'm sorry," Gregg's gruff voice brought her head up again. "It's been a long week."

"I know," Karen said. "It hasn't been easy for me, either. I went home for a funeral—" she broke off, as it registered who she was talking to.

His glance flew to her face. "And then you saw this." His eyes closed briefly. "No wonder it got to you."

She nodded, swallowing hard.

"Whose funeral?" he asked after a moment, his voice gentle.

She shook her head. Tears fell now, hot silent tears that coursed down her cheeks. If she didn't answer, maybe he would go away.

"Karen—" She felt him beside her and then his hands were on her shoulders, reaching to tilt her face up. His thumbs brushed at the tears and her eyes opened, only to close again as the last of her defenses collapsed. She felt him draw her close and his arms close around her. He pressed her head against his shoulder as great racking sobs shuddered through her.

"My mother," Karen said sometime later. She sat in the cab of his truck, leaning back against the headrest. Gregg stood in the open door with one foot resting on the running board.

He looked up. "I'm sorry."

She shrugged. "We weren't close. At least, not as close as I would have liked, but one makes choices." She opened her eyes. "I have a feeling you'd have gotten along great with her. She didn't approve of me, either." She swallowed, still too vulnerable to keep the hurt out of her voice.

Gregg looked down at her, his dark blue eyes with their thick black lashes doing very unprofessional things to her pulse rate. Karen straightened, trying to push her hair into some semblance of order, wondering if she'd ever looked worse.

Gregg's lips twitched. "Don't worry, I won't tell," he teased her. "Besides, I like my women a little disheveled."

Karen caught his glance and let her hand fall with a sigh. "I'm afraid '*a little disheveled*' doesn't quiet cover my present state."

"You know," Gregg's voice, low and conversational, caught her totally off guard, "it's possible that both your mother and I were wrong."

Her eyes flew to his face. Warmth flooded through her but she fought it down. "Don't be too quick to change your opinion. After all, you've held it for a long time. It may be deserved."

"Karen, I'm trying to apologize." His voice grated across her nerve endings.

She slipped out of the truck and walked past him. The sun had set and shadows filtered through the park. "An apology isn't necessary. I'm not proud of everything I've done. I may even deserve some of your criticism."

"Perhaps, but not the way I've treated you."

Karen could feel him close behind her but she didn't dare look at him. "I'd like to go home now. I'll see you Tuesday." She moved toward her car, opened the door, and slipped inside.

Gregg bent down to look in the open window, his face on a level with hers. He reached up to flick a single remaining tear from her cheek.

"Take care of yourself." He held her gaze for a moment before turning and walking with long strides back to his truck.

Gregg poured his third cup of coffee in less than twenty minutes and reached across to answer the intercom on his desk.

"Yes, Sue?"

"A Ms. McGraw is here to see you, sir."

Startled, he glanced at the clock. "It's only seven-thirty!"

"Shall I send her in?"

"Go ahead," he sighed.

"Good luck, sir!" He could hear the smile in Sue's voice. He walked over to the window, hoping for a moment to collect his thoughts before Karen McGraw burst in. No such luck. The door opened and he turned to see her closing it.

"Morning," he growled.

She stopped. "My, my, we really are a bear this morning, aren't we?" she chided, a smile making her eyes sparkle.

He returned to his desk. "And what gives you the right to be so offensively cheerful at this hour."

She grinned. "It's a trade secret. It throws people off guard."

"That I can believe."

"May I set down?"

"Of course. Coffee?"

"No, thanks." She looked up. "But please, have yours."

He frowned into his cup. "It doesn't seem to be helping."

"I'm sorry." She studied him for a moment.

"Yes," he said after brief pause, "I'm having trouble sleeping. I have a niece and nephew about the age of those kids. They're twins. This accident hit a little too close to home."

"I understand." She closed the note book she had opened. "We can talk about this some other time—"

"No." She started to rise and his words stopped her. "You have bothered to come all the way over here. The least I can do is—what? Am I talking or listening?"

She shifted in her chair. "Well, I didn't have anything else to do this weekend, so I sort of started without you."

"Started without me," he repeated. "What does that mean?"

"Well, I went back and looked over the crash site, just in case you might have missed something."

"Three of us scoured the place," Gregg said. "But go on."

"Well, I thought perhaps you might not have been looking for the same thing I was."

"And what might that have been?"

"I wasn't sure. Anything out of place. Anything that fit. I didn't know, but I felt I would know it when I found it." She watched his reaction.

"And you found it?"

"Maybe. There are a couple of other things, first."

"Go on."

Karen drew in her breath. "The car. Was enough left to identify it?"

"There always seems to be enough left to identify an automobile," Gregg said. "Those guys are nothing short of miracle workers."

"Then I'll leave that part to you." She drew another deep breath. "I went over to the coroner's yesterday."

Gregg set his cup down and coffee sloshed into the saucer. "You what?" He glared across his desk at her.

"Well, you weren't here for me to ask. I wasn't sure if he would talk to me, but thought I'd take a chance. We've worked together before."

"And what has he found out? I haven't had time to call this morning." He glanced at his watch. "His office isn't open yet, anyway."

Karen stood up to pace the room. "You know the young girl wasn't—well, she was thrown from the car and found just on the perimeter of the fire. The tissue damage wasn't as bad as on the other victim. He thinks a forensic artist can probably do a decent drawing. He's calling one in today."

Gregg swallowed. "Go on."

Karen twisted her hands together. "She was wearing an ankle bracelet—with a name on it."

Gregg shot to his feet. "How could I have missed that?" His breath hissed harshly from his lungs.

"Well, it was rather embedded—some of the metal had melted to her flesh—" Karen put a hand to her mouth, unable to go on.

Without thinking, Gregg went around the desk, put his hands on her arms. He looked into her face, saw her lips tremble.

"Karen, you have more guts than I would ever have believed."

Gregg's quiet voice, filled with respect, soothed and strengthened her. She drew in her breath, tried to smile.

"Two compliments in as many meetings! I'm not sure I can handle that kind of praise." She raised her eyes to his.

Gregg's eyes were hooded, his expression unreadable.

A shudder ran through her. "I don't know if I can go on with this. You warned me it would be hard—"

He leaned against his desk. "I need you on this, Karen. You made more progress this weekend than I made all last week. I don't have the time to devote to a proper investigation. I got the impression that maybe you did." His eyes searched hers. "Am I right?"

She nodded, trapped in his gaze. "Yes. I took a leave of absence to settle my mother's affairs. I haven't reported back to work yet. I thought I'd wait until this is resolved."

"Then say you're with me. Please, Karen."

She studied him, heard the husky tone of his voice as he pleaded with her. Given a choice, she could never deny him anything. At the same time, she knew just being around him would prove dangerous. Not physically—that didn't frighten her. But her emotions were already far too compromised where Gregg Watson was concerned.

She nodded. "Just promise you'll be around if I need—if it gets to be too much." She meant it as a joke, but a catch in her voice betrayed her.

"Anytime," Gregg replied, his voice almost a whisper, his magnetic blue eyes holding hers. "What else did you find?"

Karen turned from him and paced a few steps. "She landed facing away from the fire and part of her skirt that was trapped between her body and the ground didn't burn." She looked back at Gregg. "There was a pocket in the skirt and I found a couple of pieces of paper in it." She swallowed.

"What kind of paper?" Gregg asked.

"A business card from a doctor and a prescription."

Gregg stared at her. "Go on. Were you able to make out the name on the prescription?"

Karen shook her head. "I found another business card at the crash site. It's charred, but we think we can re-image it and make out the name."

"So what's next?" Gregg asked.

Karen picked up her bag. "I'm going to have a prescription filled."

"Couldn't you just ask a pharmacist to translate it?" Gregg asked.

"I could, but if they suspected it wasn't for me, I doubt if they would tell me anything. I can't make any sense of the writing. Doctors must have a code that only pharmacists understand. Anyway, I'll see what happens."

"Meet me for lunch," Gregg invited.

She shook her head. "Sorry. I'm driving over to Mason's Point."

"What's at Mason's Point?"

"A doctor. And if I can come up with a name from the prescription, I may have something to discuss with him." She held Gregg's glance for a moment, then turned and left.

CHAPTER TWO

Wednesday came and went and Gregg sat at his desk, trying to summon the interest to go home. He had made a small dent in the paperwork on his desk, but the crash remained at the edge of his thoughts. Karen McGraw had not been in touch with him since leaving his office the previous morning.

He stood up and turned a key to lock his desk, then dropped it into his pocket. His phone began ringing, the sound harsh in the empty room. He picked up the receiver.

Karen had just pushed open the door to Gregg's office when she heard his phone ring. She stopped as his voice reached her.

"Hi, sweetheart!" She hadn't imagined his voice could be so tender. "Of course, love, anytime." He leaned against his desk, the phone cradled against his shoulder. Karen pulled the door closed, and turned away.

Time enough to see him tomorrow.

Feeling unaccountably bereft, she returned to the parking lot and got into her car.

When Karen McGraw walked into his office at midmorning on Thursday, Gregg shot to his feet, staring at her. He went around the desk.

"What have I done to you?" He took in the dark circles under her eyes, the pinched look to her face. "You look like—well, you look terrible!"

"No, really," she protested, dropping her bag on a chair. "It isn't just this. It's my mother—and everything. I thought this would be a distraction. That was the main reason I agreed to help."

"I shouldn't have insisted—" Gregg began.

"I think I'm in too deep to back out now," Karen said, raising troubled eyes to his. Gregg met them for a moment, then returned to his chair.

"You have something else?" he asked.

"A little."

"Well?"

Karen swallowed. "We made out the name on the ankle bracelet. It matches the name on the prescription."

"Go on."

"The doctor who wrote the prescription was the same one whose name was on the business card."

"Did you go to see him—or her?" Gregg asked.

"I drove over and parked outside the clinic. I decided to make a phone call before I went inside."

Gregg waited.

Karen stood up and walked to a window, moving the blinds aside to look out. "I wanted to know if they had made out the name and address on the other business card," she said. "Remember? The charred one."

"You thought there might be a connection?"

"Oh, there's a connection, all right!" Karen's voice turned bitter. "Dr. Antonia Fumara's clinic is in a seedy part of town in a run down building with shutters hanging from the windows, rats scurrying across the steps—" She shivered and wrapped her arms across her chest.

"And you went inside?" Gregg stared at her.

"No. Not yet. But I think Julie did."

"*Julie!*" Gregg stood, running a hand through his hair, his eyes not leaving Karen's, his look incredulous.

"Well, yes," Karen said. "That was the name on the prescription and the bracelet—"

Gregg sat down heavily. He drew a hand across his face. "I know this is probably a long shot," he said, his voice low and controlled, "but I got a call from my niece last night. She's in college—MacKenzie State. She just returned there from spring break a few days ago. One of her friends has a younger sister who has been missing for a little over a week. Kelly didn't call expecting me to be able to do anything. She just needed to talk." He drew a deep breath. "The girl's name is Julie."

Karen stood frozen, staring at Gregg in stunned silence. When she spoke again her voice sounded wooden. "The sign over the building where Dr. Fumara has her practice reads *New Beginnings Clinic*. Her business card says she is both an obstetrician and a gynecologist. I called about the business card because I had been able to make out New and part of Beginnings. I was right."

She looked at Gregg. "It's an abortion clinic and the prescription was for an extremely powerful pain killer."

Gregg stood up. "Karen, I didn't intend you to get so involved. We just needed to identify them."

She turned away. "There's more." He saw her shiver. "The coroner did blood tests on them—to help with identification. It was difficult with the young man—because of the condition of the body, but it should've been a simple procedure with Julie."

Karen turned back, her eyes tragic. "Gregg—" she whispered. He reached for her, drew her into his arms. He felt a tremulous sigh course through her slender body.

"He had such a hard time getting blood he did some checking." Karen brought a hand to her mouth. "He thinks she probably hemorrhaged and died before the crash." Her voice sounded brittle, tight with control.

Gregg stared at her, wordless.

"There's one other thing." Karen wet her lips. "She wore a St. Christopher's metal."

Gregg turned away. "Did the coroner confirm the abortion?"

"Oh, yes." Karen's voice turned matter-of-fact. "He thinks she was well into her fifth month."

When Gregg spoke again his voice was bitter. "Young, in trouble, Catholic." His gaze swung back to Karen. "Are you thinking what I'm thinking?"

"That clinics like *New Beginnings* that deal in late term abortions are slaughter houses? I intend to find out." Karen had herself under control now, her voice firm and sure.

Gregg's head came up to look at her. He wanted to argue, but this was not the time. Instead he asked, "What more do we need before we have a positive identification?"

"A lot." Karen said, all business now. "I don't have much faith in the last name, under the circumstances—even if I go to the clinic and find a record of her visit, which I doubt I will. Have you made any progress on the car?"

"Yes, and no." Gregg raked a dark lock of hair off his forehead. "They traced it to a Father Brian McFeld. However, his sister says he's been doing missionary work in Central America for several months and won't be home for several more. She talked to him night before last."

"So the car is stolen?" Karen asked.

"It hasn't been reported. Miss McFeld promised to call back if she can get in touch with her brother and comes up with any leads that might help."

Karen sat down. "I have to go back to the clinic. Maybe there will be records—"

Gregg shook his head. "I can't let you go back there alone."

Karen glanced up. "Do you think you can stop me?"

His lips twitched. "I wouldn't dream of trying. I'll go with you."

She caught her breath. "Of course you won't. You don't have time, remember? That's why I'm helping—"

"We'll go in the morning," he said, getting to his feet. "Bring an overnight bag."

She stared at him, the color draining from her face. "I couldn't stay there—" she wet her lips.

"Not there," Gregg said. "I'm taking you to the ranch for the weekend. You need a break—"

"I couldn't possibly—" Karen protested automatically, unconscious of the wistful expression that crossed her face.

"Of course you can," he persisted. "Kelly and Kyle will be there, along with my mother and the housekeeper, so we'll be very adequately chaperoned. I asked Kelly to bring a picture of Julie." His voice faded.

Karen looked at him. "Did you suspect last night?"

"Not really. I told her to bring the picture to give her something to do. I hope—as selfish as it sounds—that this is just coincidence."

"Why is that selfish?" Karen asked, looking at him.

"Kelly is very close to her friend's family. She and Kyle lost their mother—my sister—almost three years ago. She doesn't need any more tragedy—not that anyone else does, either." He ran a hand through his hair again. "In this business it's always easier if the bodies remain statistics. That's where the selfish part comes in."

"Gregg." Karen touched his arm, her voice husky with emotion. She held his gaze, trying to think of something to say. At last she shrugged. "You're only human, after all."

Something flashed in his eyes and he gently mocked her. "Such an endorsement, and from the almighty Karen McGraw, no less! I'll bet you didn't think that a week ago."

"Well, I've had doubts over the years." A smile touched the corners of her mouth. "But I have it on good authority that you do have a heart."

"We'll leave at seven in the morning," he said. "Meet me here—"

She shook her head. "Too early. The clinic doesn't open until ten and it's only a two hour drive."

"Then we'll have time for breakfast, won't we?" He picked up her bag and adjusted it over her shoulder. "See you at seven."

Karen glared at him for a moment. "Why do I feel like I should salute?" she asked over her shoulder as she headed for the door.

Gregg grinned and waved, wincing as the door closed with a bit more force than necessary. He dropped back into his chair, the smile fading as he passed a tired hand over his face.

Dear God, don't let this be a dead end. And thanks for sending Karen to help.

"I've figured out my story," Karen said as she got into her car the next morning. They decided it would be the more comfortable vehicle for the drive.

"What story?" Gregg asked as he studied the set of keys in his hand.

Karen took the ring from him, selected a key and removed it with a deft twist. She handed it to him and dropped the rest into her bag.

"Is that because you don't trust me, or because you don't have much faith in my ability to remember which key is which?" He started the car and turned out of the parking lot.

She shrugged. "Maybe a little of both. Maybe neither."

"What story?" he asked again after a brief pause.

"My cover. About why I need an abortion. And why I chose *New Beginnings.*"

She heard Gregg's indrawn breath as he turned to stare at her.

"Gregg, please, the road."

He turned back. "I didn't realize you needed a story."

"Maybe I won't, but I thought I should be prepared, just in case."

"Just in case, what?" he asked, frowning.

"In case the only way I can get the information I need is to pretend I need the services of the clinic. I can gush on about how someone named Julie recommended it—I won't quite be able to remember her last name, though. Maybe they will slip up and give it to me. If not, I have a few other tricks."

"So what is it?" Gregg asked when she paused.

"What is what?"

"Your story?"

"Well, a clinic like this either does abortions because the pregnancy is too far advanced for a reputable doctor to take on, or because someone wants it kept very, very secret. In Julie's case, it was both. In my case, it will be secrecy. Since my husband is a prominent banker in our small town, who just happens to be sterile from an illness he suffered in his early twenties, I don't want him to know about my lover, do I? Which he most certainly will, now that I'm pregnant—" Karen broke off as she saw a muscle twitch in Gregg's jaw. "Think it'll work?"

"Is that story a reflection of your values?" His voice sounded hard and bitter, with no room for compromise.

Karen cringed, but held her head high. "I don't think that deserves an answer." Her lashes fell and she turned to look out the window.

Gregg fell silent, knowing he had hurt her, but not quite knowing what to do about it. The silence stretched on and he knew she wouldn't be the one to break it. He sighed.

"Do you always go to such lengths to get your story?" he asked.

He felt her glance. "If I answer, do I get to ask you a question?"

He shrugged. "What could you possibly want to know? My life's an open book."

27

"No one's life's an open book!" Karen replied. "Yes or no?"

"To what? Oh, your question. Sure. Why not?"

"Okay, to answer your question, I do whatever it takes to get a story—if it's worth getting. To date, nothing I've done has come near this in importance. I'm prepared to go further, if necessary."

"Meaning what?" He frowned.

"I think it's my turn," Karen said. She paused to pull her thoughts into focus. "I know your job is hard. I know you see and hear a lot of things that no one should see. You have to keep them in perspective—as statistics—if you will." She stopped, drew a deep breath, and plunged on. "Is that why, every time I think I see a side of you that approaches humanity, you have to slap me back? Because in exposing those feelings, you become vulnerable. You could be hurt." She sighed. "Or is it just me—or rather, your opinion of me?"

"After all that," he growled, "I need a translator."

She turned to stare at him for a long moment. Then she closed her eyes and leaned back against the seat.

"Never mind," she said, pressing her lips together to keep them from trembling. "I think I'll try and get a little more sleep since you're driving." Fat chance, she told herself. But if her eyes were closed, maybe he wouldn't try to talk. If he wasn't talking, he couldn't say anything that would hurt.

Gregg looked at her and then back to the road. Why did he always do this to her? She'd arrived at his office looking particularly enchanting in a green silk blouse and slim black slacks. Her rich brown hair and vivid coloring seemed even more vibrant than usual, her dark eyes sparkling beneath a thick fringe of lashes. He glanced at her again. In repose she looked fragile, helpless almost. His mouth twisted. Not likely! Or was she? He looked back and found himself grinding his teeth to keep from groaning.

Looking ahead he saw a rest stop and pulled off the road. He cut the engine and sat for a moment before turning to face her. Her eyes were still closed, but the tear he'd seen sliding down her cheek a moment before had now been joined by several others.

"Why did we stop?" She did not open her eyes.

"Suppose you tell me." Gregg caught her chin and turned her face to his. Her eyes opened, the black lashes drenched and sparkling with tears.

"Look," Gregg said, his voice gruff, "I know I can be a self-righteous jerk. You know that, too. So don't take it so personally, okay?"

Karen shook her head. "It isn't just you," she denied. "I was thinking about my mother. She didn't like me much, either."

"Karen!" With a groan Gregg reached for her and pulled her onto his lap. "What am I going to do with you?" he asked, his lips against her hair.

Karen nestled into his warmth and strength, powerless to deny herself this haven. "Why do you have to do anything?" she whispered, one hand resting against his chest.

"Because you're getting under my skin, that's why," he growled. "I knew I was taking a chance when I suggested you help me. Somehow, I thought I would be stronger—" His voice trailed off.

"Gregg, look at me!" Karen stared at him. "Now I need a translator!"

He grinned and lifted her back into her seat. "Are you feeling better?"

She met his eyes. "Should I be?"

He turned away to start the engine. "Don't play games, sweetheart," he drawled. "I don't make a worthy opponent."

Karen leaned back and closed her eyes again. "If you only knew," she murmured under her breath.

"Well, here goes." Karen reached to open the door. "Wish me luck."

"Of course." Gregg looked at her for a moment, then bent and brushed his lips against hers. "Take care."

She stared at him, more shaken than she wanted to admit. She stepped out of the car, then turned and walked up the shabby steps.

The *New Beginnings Clinic* was worse than she remembered from the day before, perhaps because then she had only observed it from a distance. Now, up close and personal, she was about to step inside, to God only knew what. She pushed open the door.

A blurred figure moved behind a desk. "Are you girl from temporary agency?" The feminine voice had a heavy Eastern accent.

Karen waited for her eyes to adjust to the dimness after the bright sunlight. That also gave her a moment to think.

"Yes," she lied after a moment's hesitation, with only a slight twinge of guilt. "I wasn't sure this was the place."

"I only need you until one-thirty today. My regular girl called in ill. I need someone to answer phone, pull up records on computer. You are familiar with computer?"

Karen nodded, afraid to trust her voice. "I can handle the job," she assured the woman. "May I just tell my ride that this is the place, and to pick me up at one-thirty?"

"Please hurry. I have much to do."

Dear Father, thank you for this break. Please let me find the information I need.

Gregg was leaning against the car when Karen ran down the steps. He turned to meet her, catching her arms as she rushed up to him.

"What happened? That didn't take long. Are you—?"

"I don't have time to explain. She thinks I'm from a temporary agency. I'm to answer the phone and pull up computer records. Come back for me at one-thirty."

"I can't leave you here!" Gregg exploded, his look incredulous.

"Of course you can. I've been taking care of myself for a long time. You might help me out by hanging around and trying to divert the real temporary. On second thought, I can do that myself if one shows up."

"You're crazy!"

"Probably. Actually, this was what I had in mind from the beginning—access to the computer records. I just had no real idea how to get to them. I know this sounds too easy. Perhaps it is. I have a phone in the car. I'll call if things don't work out."

"I'll wait around the corner for a few minutes in case you change your mind," Gregg said. He realized the futility of arguing with her. And she was right, after all. She couldn't pass up an opportunity that appeared to have dropped from the sky. "Be careful, will you?"

She grinned. "Of course. I'm always careful!" She saw his eyes flash in disbelief and turned away. "I have to run. I hear a phone ringing and my boss has 'much to do'." She hurried up the steps and through the door.

Gregg stared after her. What was he supposed to do now? He glanced at his watch. He could play along with Karen's theory and check around town to see if anyone remembered seeing two teenagers in a light blue metallic late model Buick on the day of the crash.

CHAPTER THREE

Gregg pulled up before the clinic at exactly one-thirty, his face grim. Karen was no where to be seen. He got out of the car to pace. Should he go inside and check on her? Just as he'd decided he couldn't wait any longer, the door opened and he heard her voice as she replied to someone inside.

"I'm supposed to start another assignment on Monday," Karen was saying. "If that falls through, I'll let you know. I enjoyed working here. It's been very informative." She closed the door and came unhurriedly down the steps, her face becoming guarded as she read Gregg's thunderous expression.

Gregg caught her shoulders. "I've been worried to death about you, and here you're about to begin a new career!"

"Don't be ridiculous," Karen said. "I couldn't burn my bridges behind me." She opened her bag to reveal a diskette. "I don't know if I got everything

I needed."

His eyes narrowed. "I'm not sure how many laws you've broken this morning, but I feel I should be charging you with something." He opened the car door and she climbed inside. Back in the driver's seat, he threw her a dark look. "I'll just have to make sure I don't let you out of my sight."

"And how do you propose to do that?" Karen challenged.

"You're coming out to the ranch for the weekend."

"You said that before. I can't. I didn't bring a bag." She wanted to go, Karen admitted to herself. In fact, she wanted it too much. That's why she'd made herself forget about his offer.

"I know. I didn't trust you so I searched the car. We'll just have to stop and pick up your things." His voice was cool, hard, and determined.

Karen studied him. "Don't you know how to take no for an answer?" she asked, baiting him.

"I've never had to," he said. "Would it still compromise whatever code you live by if I were to tell you that I need you at the ranch this weekend?"

"How can you need me?" Karen's voice went harsh.

"I told you Kelly will be there. She was close to Julie. You might find out something that will help." He paused. "She may be able to help you, too."

"Help me?" Karen looked up. "In what way?"

"She lost her mother three years ago. If you need someone to talk to, I know she's a good listener."

"Like you, perhaps?" Karen threw at him.

He sighed and she heard his teeth snap together. "On second thought, if you intend to judge my whole family by what you believe me to be, maybe you should stay home and wallow in self-pity all weekend." His knuckles

33

whitened where he gripped the steering wheel and Karen could feel his anger as if it were a living presence.

Karen fell silent as her pride lost a battle with her desire. She raised her head and put a hand on his arm. "I'm sorry. I'd love to go. I left my bag in your office before you got there. I wasn't sure how serious you were."

"Do I strike you as someone who makes idle gestures?" he grated.

She shook her head. "No. I doubt if you've ever said anything you didn't mean. That's why this new Gregg Watson takes a little getting used to."

"Karen—" he broke off. Then, "How about telling me about your *'very informative'* morning?" he suggested.

She gave an exaggerated sigh. "I thought you'd never ask. Everything I suspected was more or less confirmed. She performed three procedures this morning—that's the current politically correct term for abortion. Friday is a very popular day. The patients have the weekend to recover."

"Exactly what was it you suspected?" Gregg asked.

"First, that Dr. Fumara is performing late term abortions that other doctors won't touch. In her patient database, she even lists the stage at termination. I paged through it and at least a third were past mid-term."

"In some third world countries, abortion is the primary means of birth control. Timing—is irrelevant. Maybe Dr. Fumara thinks that way.".

She swallowed. "In this case, one abortion may have cost two lives, maybe three. I have to determine whether or not the state of Julie's health was a factor in the crash."

"Why do you think it might be a factor?"

"Well, the scenario I see is two nice kids, from good families, who care about each other. They got careless and she's pregnant. What to do? There's no one they can talk to. Their religion, at least hers, prohibits abortion. They don't want to embarrass their families. They hear about this clinic, a few hundred miles away. They decide a good way to spend their spring break is to drive down and take care of the problem. Only something goes tragically wrong. Either Julie is too young, or her pregnancy too far advanced. She wasn't kept at the clinic for observation long enough. As they are driving away, she starts having problems. It must have been fairly soon. They hadn't had time to fill her prescription—or perhaps she was already so medicated she didn't feel the pain—didn't realize she was hemorrhaging until it was too late."

Karen was silent for a few seconds. "From there, I can see two possibilities. The driver might have been distracted by Julie's difficulties and lost control of the car trying to help her."

"Or?" Gregg prompted, turning his head to glance at her.

"Or, realizing that she was dead, and not knowing how to face her parents or his, or life without her, he used the car to commit suicide." Her voice was hard and flat.

Gregg drew in his breath. "I guess my profession isn't the only one that exposes the seedy underbelly of polite society." He made his voice deliberately cold, crude.

"Gregg!" Karen gasped.

"I did a little snooping while you played receptionist," he said. "I think you're too close to the truth for comfort."

"What do you mean?" Karen stared at Gregg.

"Instead of waiting for you, I decided to ask around town, see if anyone might have seen these kids—or the car. I figured the car would be the best bet. According to Miss McFeld, it was a light blue metallic. The first filling station I stopped at, I hit pay dirt. The attendant remembered the car—and Julie."

"I imagine she was very beautiful," Karen said.

"Probably. But that wasn't what he remembered." Something in Gregg's voice made Karen look at him.

"What then?"

"He said she was very ill—as white as a sheet, to quote him. She said she felt sick and went into the bathroom. He could hear her throwing up. Shortly after they left, another customer reported that the bathroom was a mess—blood everywhere. He said he didn't know how anyone could have lost that much blood and still be alive. He had the license number from the credit card purchase and he called the police and reported the incident." Gregg reached in his pocket. "That's the license number of the car, and the name on the credit card." He handed her a scrap of paper.

Karen looked at it, puzzled. "Brian McFeld. We already knew that."

"We knew the car was his. Who did he also trust with his credit card?"

"If he was going to be gone for several months, perhaps he had a local boy, probably someone from his church, take care of the car for him. You know, drive it occasionally, wash it." She glanced at Gregg. "Did you get a description of the young man from the attendant?"

"Slender, dark hair. Seemed distracted. Didn't talk much. About seventeen. He guessed the girl to be fifteen or sixteen."

"And what did she look like?"

"Blonde, fair. Enormous blue eyes. About five foot three." His jaw clenched. "The exact description of our Julie."

"Dear God!" Karen whispered.

"If Kelly brings a picture, I'll bring it over on Monday to see if the gas station attendant can make a positive identification. Who knows, Kelly may even know her boyfriend!" Gregg gave a ragged sigh, harsh in the strained silence. Karen sat helplessly, feeling his pain as well as her own. She had allowed herself to get far too involved, in more ways than one.

"I'll come with you," she offered.

He shook his head. "I'd rather you didn't. Your job is finished—"

"Not until we have a positive identification," she said, her lips trembling. "How can you just throw me back like this—now that you don't need me—"

"I'm thinking of your feelings."

"Then don't. I told you I can take care of myself!" She turned away, then looked back at him. "Oh, I get it! I might get to see the human side of Gregg Watson. God forbid that should happen!"

She saw a muscle twitch in his tightly clenched jaw. "Okay, you can come. Actually, this sort of thing is probably right up your alley. It should provide you with a few kicks—"

She drew in her breath harshly, staring at him. She knew she had left herself open to his contempt by pushing him too far. Something fragile and vulnerable inside of her shrank in upon itself and died. She turned away to stare out the window, not deigning to reply.

Dear God, please help Gregg. Let him find peace, and don't let me add to his burdens. And if possible, let me help him.

The remainder of the drive seemed endless until at last Gregg pulled her car into the parking lot of the police station. He cut the engine and turned to look at her.

"Please come out to the ranch," he pleaded. "I need you."

Karen gasped. "How can you even ask—"

"I know I was unfair. I'm sorry."

"Is that all you can say?"

"No. There's a lot more. I just don't know if any of it will do me any good now."

She shrugged. "Try it. What have you got to lose?"

That brought a small twitch to his mouth, as if he tried not to smile. He ran a hand through his hair.

"It's been two weeks today since I found them." His voice grew quiet. "No case has ever haunted me the way this one has. Now that it's almost over, it may become even more personal. It's not much of an excuse, but it's the best I can do." He opened the door and stepped out.

Karen sat frozen as he came around to open her door. She climbed out and turned to him. "I understand, Gregg," she said. "I understand so much more than you're willing to give me credit for!"

When he didn't answer, or look at her, she reached out to touch his face. He raised his head and she walked up to him, sliding her arms under his jacket, around his waist. She rested her cheek against his chest.

"Please know that I'm here, Gregg, if I can do anything!"

He stood tensely, looking down at her. He wanted to put his arms around her, but he didn't trust himself. He might never let her go. Her voice was muffled against his chest, and he raised a hand to touch her hair.

She stirred. "Gregg?"

"Hmmm?"

"I'd love to spend the weekend at your ranch, meet your niece and nephew. Is that invitation still good?"

"For at least another five minutes," he said, and she could hear a smile in his voice. She relaxed fractionally and raised her head.

"Then what are we waiting for?"

"I have to check my messages and clock out, and get your bag." He glanced at his watch. "That should take all of ten minutes, at most."

Karen decided to wait for Gregg in the parking lot and enjoy the perfect afternoon. She leaned against her car, her face upturned to the cooling breeze, and tried to relax. *Tried not to think about this impossible, maddening, wonderful man who had somehow managed to turn her life into total chaos.* A chaos that she believed to somehow be a part of God's plan for her life.

After a while, Karen realized she'd been standing there for quite some time. She glanced at her watch. Fifteen minutes since Gregg went inside. She'd give him a little longer. He probably had more messages than he anticipated.

After another fifteen minutes Karen began pacing. Something had happened. She crossed the parking lot to the main building where Gregg had his office.

Karen knocked then pushed open the door. Gregg sat behind his desk, his chair turned to face the wall. She couldn't see his face, but she could see that he rested his chin on a clenched fist.

"Gregg—" she said.

He spun around in his chair. "What are you doing here?"

"I got worried. Something happened." She went toward him. "Didn't it?" She could see his face now—drawn and haggard. Without thinking she moved to stand beside him. "Talk to me, Gregg!"

He shook his head, then reached for her. Her hands came up to stroke his hair, offering comfort as she felt him tremble. He drew a deep breath.

"Miss McFeld called," his voice sounded wooden as he struggled with emotion. "A young man took care of her brother's car in return for limited use of it. She took the liberty of contacting the authorities before calling me. He's been missing for over a week. He never returned home after spring break."

CHAPTER FOUR

Karen stood on a balcony overlooking the lake and watched entranced as a small airplane came in for a landing. The airstrip paralleled the lake and the windsock indicated a slight breeze straight down the runway. The plane made a perfect touch down and taxied up to the hangar. The engine stopped and the propeller spun down. Gregg came out of the house and walked with long strides toward the plane.

The door opened and a young man stepped down, then turned back and helped a girl from the plane. Seeing Gregg, she immediately threw herself into his arms. Then, his arm around her shoulder, they turned back to the house, leaving the young man to put the plane away.

Karen saw Gregg stop and turn to the girl. She was explaining something, her gestures animated. Karen couldn't hear their voices, but she could see that whatever he heard was having a profound effect on Gregg. He ran a restless hand through his hair, then turned and looked toward the window of Karen's room. Seeing her on the balcony he raised a hand in greeting. The girl turned and saw Karen for the first time. She turned back to Gregg. Whatever she said to him made him laugh. He put his arm around her again, and they went into the house.

"Karen!" Gregg's voice and a pounding on her door startled Karen a few minutes later. She had changed into jeans and freed her hair from the braid that had confined it all day. She put down her brush and hurried to the door.

Gregg waited impatiently, his hand raised to knock again when Karen pulled the door open.

"Julie's back," he said, brushing past Karen and then turning back to face her from the middle of the room.

Karen stared at him and then closed the door carefully.

"Isn't that—good?" she asked.

"What? Of course, it is. It's just—" he hesitated.

"That we're back to square one," Karen finished for him. She walked over to the window. "What happened? Where has she been?"

"Spring break, as we suspected. She left with friends, but she had them drop her off at a camp of some kind. They were supposed to go on to the beach for a few days and pick her up on the way back. When they didn't show up, she had to make other arrangements to return. She didn't call home because she knew her parents were out of town and she didn't realize her sister had returned early."

"What happened to her friends?" Karen asked, her voice quiet.

Gregg looked at her. "Now I know why you're a reporter and I'm not," he said. "I was so relieved about Julie that I never thought to ask about the others." He ran a hand through his hair. "I'll ask Kelly." He held her gaze for a moment. "Of course you realize this is a long shot."

She nodded. "It just happens to be all we have at the moment." She continued to look out the window, her arms clasped across her chest, her hands rubbing her upper arms.

"Come here," Gregg said gruffly.

Her head jerked up, alerted by something in his voice. She wet her lips. "I beg your pardon?"

"I said come here. I need to hold you." His voice was tender, with just a trace of huskiness.

Karen stood as if rooted, her dark eyes enormous. "I don't think that's such a good idea!"

He snapped his fingers. "And it was the best one I've had today!" He shrugged, a masterpiece of casual elegance. "Maybe next time."

Karen couldn't take her eyes off him. When he tried, he had the sexiest smile she'd ever seen. Come to think of it, he didn't even have to smile to get her attention. His mouth was the first thing she'd noticed about him. His lips were firm and chiseled. She liked the way they compressed when he tried not to smile. Not that he'd been inclined to smile then. He had been so angry with her, having just rescued her from a street gang. Even as he stood glaring down at her, she'd fought the urge to reach up and trace his lips with her finger tip.

Karen realized she was staring at Gregg, and pulled herself together with an effort. "When do I get to meet everyone?" she asked. "I assume that was your niece and nephew in the plane?"

He nodded. "They both fly. You'll have to get one of them to take you up. The ranch is impressive from the air."

"It's impressive from the ground," Karen said with feeling. "It must have been in your family for generations."

"Four." His expression became distant. "Unfortunately, now there's only me and the twins to enjoy all this. A rather sad fate for my great-grandfather's legacy."

Karen frowned. "Why so negative? The twins can still have kids, and you, too. You aren't all that ancient," she teased with a smile.

He grinned. "No? Well, unless I get started soon, I'll have grandchildren, or rather grand nieces and nephews, older than my children."

"I think that sounds wonderful," Karen said, her voice wistful. "The only relative I got to keep was my mother."

Gregg looked at her for a moment, started to speak, then changed his mind. "I think I heard Mom's car," he said. "Ready to go down?"

Whatever expectations she had concerning Gregg's mother, Karen discarded them immediately upon being introduced to her. The slender vivacious blonde in her late fifties was anything but work worn and weather-beaten. She looked more like a professional model than a ranch wife, at least the way Karen had pictured it.

The twins were exactly what she expected. They were smaller replicas of Gregg, both exceptionally attractive. They were identical—or as identical as they could be. Kelly was a few inches shorter than Kyle, more slender, and most definitely feminine.

And Kyle. Looking at him, Karen caught her breath. His laughing blue eyes and smiling lips made her long to see that side of Gregg. Then she caught herself. He was hard enough to resist at his cynical worst. If he should decide to turn on the charm, she'd be lost.

"My dear, welcome to our home!" Anna Watson caught Karen's hands in greeting. "Gregg said you're a reporter. I so admire anyone with the tenacity to make it in such a competitive profession. I once had aspirations toward a media career, but was scared off. Are you comfortable? Did Gregg get you settled in properly?"

"Oh, yes. Perfect!" Karen said, redirecting her thoughts to meet Anna's abrupt change of subject. Unable to stop herself, Karen glanced up to meet Gregg's eyes, correctly interpreting the look he threw her way. He was laughing at her, enjoying her discomfiture, as she reassessed his mother. She turned back to Anna. "Thank you for making me so welcome. You have a beautiful home."

"Thank you," Anna replied with a warm smile. "We try not to take it for granted. Sometimes it's hard—since we've all grown up here." She looked at Gregg. "Have you had a chance to show Karen around?"

"Not yet. We just got here."

"Why don't you take her down to the lake while I check with Marie about dinner?" Anna suggested.

Gregg looked at Karen. "How about it? Tomorrow Kelly wants you to go riding and Kyle plans to take you flying. This may be my only chance."

"Sounds like fun," Karen said. "I saw the lake from my balcony. Does it have a name?"

Gregg and Anna exchanged glances and Anna laughed before turning away. "I'll let you field that one, Gregg!" she said over her shoulder.

"What did I say?" Karen turned back to Gregg.

He grinned. "Did I tell you my great-grandfather was a Scot?" he asked, taking her arm to lead her from the house.

As soon as Gregg and Karen left the room, Kelly and Kyle materialized at Anna's side. Kelly's eyes were shining.

"Gram, is this it? Is Uncle Gregg in love?" she asked.

"If he isn't, he must be crazy as well as blind," Kyle put in dryly.

"My dears, you only just met her!" Anna reminded, her eyes twinkling.

"But she's perfect!" Kelly protested. "How long do you have to know someone to realize that?"

"I like her, too," Anna admitted. "And I would say she must be special for Gregg to bring her here. But you know there isn't anyone better than he is at hiding what he thinks or feels. I don't have a clue."

"How did he explain her?" Kelly persisted.

"He said they're working on a case. He needs to use your computer later tonight, Kyle. He wanted me to ask in case you disappeared before he had a chance."

"Sure. No problem. But, actually, I wasn't planning on going anywhere. I have a report due next week."

"What about you, Kelly?" Anna asked. "What are your plans for the weekend?"

"Nothing special," Kelly said. "I just wanted to come home, see you and Uncle Gregg. After the scare we all had over Julie, I guess I needed reassurance."

Anna drew her close, kissed the shining head. "I'm glad you're here," she whispered. She put an arm out to Kyle and he walked into her embrace. "I'm so glad you know you have me and Gregg." Her voice was husky, her eyes filled with love and sadness.

"Loch Claren," Karen repeated, her eyes sparkling as she looked up at Gregg. "But of course! Lake McClaren, or Lake of the Clarens. I like Gregory McClaren's sense of romance." She turned back toward the lake and felt a breeze touch her face and play with her hair.

Gregg saw her eyes close in pleasure and fought down the urge to reach for her. *So she liked his great-grandfather's flair for the romantic.* Maybe he'd have a chance to show her that trait had been passed down to his offspring as well. He had a lot to make up for and needed every advantage he could muster where Karen was concerned.

Karen turned back to Gregg, her lips parted to speak. The words died in her throat. A smile played around his mouth and danced in his eyes. She swallowed convulsively.

"It does rather leave you speechless, doesn't it?" Gregg said. "I'd like to take you out in the boat, but it's a little late and you don't have a jacket. Maybe tomorrow."

"What kind of boat?" Karen forced herself to concentrate on what he was saying. She tore her eyes away from his mouth.

"Just a small speed boat. Megan and the kids liked to ski, so I bought it a few years ago, just after Rock was killed. I like to just shoot around the lake. It's my escape—or as close as I get."

"Megan?" Karen said.

"My sister." He didn't look at her.

"And Rock?" She looked at him, eyes narrowed. "What are Kelly and Kyle's last names?"

"Brantly. Rock Brantly was their father."

Karen drew in her breath painfully. "I remember the crash and the search. That was my first assignment."

Gregg looked at her, the smile gone. "That was over eight years ago."

Karen nodded, turned away. "I'd just been hired by the *Clarion* as an apprentice. A Coast Guard helicopter crash was sensational enough, but no one else had the patience to wait out the search. While I waited for some word on him, I did a lot of background research. Afterwards, sort of as therapy, I guess, I put it all together in an article called *'Death of a Hero'*. I—"

Gregg sucked in his breath. "You wrote that?" He shook his head in disbelief. "Megan found it comforting that someone could write something so sensitive at such a time."

"I used to write as K. D. McGraw," Karen said. "It was more acceptable to some people to not know I was a woman back then."

"And things are different now?" Gregg asked.

She looked at him. "For some people. Not everybody." She turned and walked back toward the house.

CHAPTER FIVE

Karen slipped the diskette into Kyle's computer and typed in a command. She looked up at a tap on the door and Kelly walked in.

"I wanted to give this to Gregg before you get too busy," Kelly said, crossing over to Karen. "It's a picture of Julie's friends. Laurie took it just before they all left together for spring break. I was going to bring him a picture of Julie. Since she's all right, I thought perhaps he could help with Matt and Juliana."

Karen's hands crashed convulsively on the keyboard and she folded them in her lap.

"Matt—and Juliana," she repeated. "What are their last names?" She took the picture Kelly held out to her.

Kelly knelt beside her. "Kelso. Matt and Juliana are brother and sister.

Juliana is Julie's best friend." As she said their names, Kelly pointed to them in the photo. "They're almost the same size, both blonde. They've been inseparable as long as anyone can remember." Kelly stood up, her eyes sad. "Will you give that to Gregg for me? I don't think he's expecting it—but he has a way of making everything right. I hoped—"

"I'll give it to him," Karen said, her throat tightening with emotion. She stood up and put her arms around Kelly. "We'll see what we can do."

When Kelly left, Karen turned back to the computer. She pulled up the files she'd loaded and began to search, this time with a purpose. From time to time she glanced at the photo lying on the desk, wondering what had happened to Gregg. Finally, she found what she was looking for, scanned it quickly, then sent it to the printer.

Karen unintentionally hit the page key just as she was getting ready to erase the file from Kyle's computer. Her eyes widened in astonishment and then closed tightly in pain for a moment. She leaned forward to look at the screen more closely.

Gregg pushed open the door to Kyle's study to find Karen standing by the window in the darkness.

"I'm sorry I took so long," he said. "I was going to help you, but I got another phone call from Miss McFeld. I meant to tell you earlier. The name of the young man taking care of her brother's car was—"

"Matt Kelso."

She heard Gregg's harsh intake of breath, felt his gaze on her in the darkness. "Matt Kelso," he confirmed with a sigh. "How did you know?"

"Kelly was looking for you. She had a picture of Julie and her friends—Matt and Juliana Kelso, brother and sister." Karen didn't look at

Gregg. She went to the desk and picked up the photo.

Gregg flipped a switch and Karen blinked in the harsh light. He took the photo from her, saw her hand tremble. He was afraid to look at her too closely, afraid the pain he heard in her voice would be reflected in her eyes. He couldn't be much comfort to her. His own pain went too deep.

Karen waited until he had looked at the photo then handed him the first page she'd printed. She began speaking, her voice a low monotone.

"Julie Ann Kendrick is the name on the prescription. The date is the same as the day of the crash, seven o'clock in the morning. Dr. Fumara likes to start early. She was released at two-thirty. I'm particularly interested in the comments *'unexpected complications'* and *'difficult patient'.*"

"Yet she released her." Gregg's voice was flat.

Karen nodded. "One little tidbit of information I managed to glean this morning is that she has no facilities for keeping patients overnight."

"How can that be?"

Karen shrugged. "I'm not sure. Some legitimate hospitals don't keep mothers overnight after they give birth. Everyone seems to be cutting costs where ever possible. She recommends that everyone have someone come with them, and if they have complications that concern them, they should go to the emergency room or their regular doctor. She merely runs an outpatient clinic."

"So she accepts no responsibility?" Gregg put his hands in his pockets. He wanted to strike someone.

"None. And her patients have no alternative. They go to her after making the decision that abortion is their only choice and for reasons we've already discussed." Karen picked up the second sheet she had printed and handed it to Gregg. "Take a look at this."

Gregg scanned the sheet, a frown creasing his brow. "Tracy Lowe? What's this all about? The date is just over a year ago."

"She worked with me. She'd just gotten the job with the *Clarion* and I was training her. She was good. I thought she could be the best." Karen walked over to the window again.

"After a few months, she started complaining about her weight. She'd gained a few pounds, but I never suspected anything. Then one day she said she wouldn't be in on Friday. She was taking a long weekend to visit her parents. That all sounded innocent enough."

Karen made a restless movement, pushed back her hair. "She didn't show up on Monday, as planned. When she still wasn't there by noon, and I couldn't reach her at home, I called her mother. She hadn't seen Tracy since the week before and asked if anything was wrong. I told her I must be mistaken about her schedule. I said I'd recheck it and apologized for bothering her."

Gregg saw Karen wrap her arms across her chest in that protective gesture he'd come to know during the past week. He wanted to pull her into his arms and shield her from all the hurt, but that was impossible and they both knew it. He couldn't comfort her now, and she had more strength than he did.

"I had a bad feeling about the whole situation. In the time I'd worked with Tracy, there'd been nothing to indicate irresponsibility. If possible, she was too conscientious. I asked my editor to go with me, and we went to her apartment. Her car was in the parking lot, parked rather haphazardly. When our knock wasn't answered, we asked the manager to let us in."

Karen drew a deep breath. "The coroner said she'd been dead since Friday night. Foul play was ruled out but I never heard a cause of death. She was twenty-two, beautiful, loving, and according to Dr. Fumara's records, six months pregnant at the time of termination."

Karen stepped out of the shower and wrapped herself in a huge towel. She felt deliciously tired and wanted nothing more than a nap. The day had started early with Kyle taking her flying before breakfast.

"In case you have a tendency to be air sick," he said with a grin. He explained that flying was smoother first thing in the morning, so she would be less likely to have problems.

After breakfast Anna took her on a complete tour of the house. Twenty plus rooms, including what had once been servant's quarters. When they returned to the kitchen, Kelly claimed Karen to take her riding. Marie packed a picnic lunch and Karen found herself being shown over what seemed hundreds of acres. She saw cattle and horses, even sheep.

Karen learned the ranch employed a surprising number of hands and was set up to run like a small corporation. Kelly explained that was the only way Gregg could manage it with all his other interests. The present foreman had worked for Gregg's father and he had complete trust in him in all matters.

Karen found both Kyle and Kelly more than willing to talk about their uncle. It was easy to see that they worshipped him. She also learned that the airplane had been owned jointly by Gregg and their father. Gregg kept it up until they were old enough to learn to fly and when they both developed a love of flying, he signed two-thirds interest in the plane over to them.

Karen returned from the ride near collapse. She'd spent a restless night after Gregg walked out of Kyle's study and secluded himself in his office. She heard him moving around far into the night. Even after he went upstairs to bed, she couldn't fall asleep.

Gregg had shut her out after her story about Tracy. Apparently her usefulness to him was over. He had what he wanted. He could identify the two teenagers and they would go their separate ways. She was grateful to Kyle and Kelly for keeping her busy. She hadn't had time to think.

Now she was exhausted. As far as she knew, nothing else was planned before dinner. She had time for a nap. She slipped on a night shirt and lay down across the bed, reaching for a cotton throw at the foot of the bed.

"Where's Karen?" Gregg poked his head into the sun room where Anna was writing.

"I believe she went upstairs to take a shower," Anna replied without looking up. "She was exhausted after she and Kelly got back from riding. I told her she had time to take a nap if she wanted to."

"Why would she be so tired?" Gregg asked with a frown.

Anna pushed back her chair and swiveled around to look at him. Her face was stern. "I expect you know the answer to that better than I do. She didn't look as if she slept well. And we had a full morning planned for her. We did our best to be good hosts—unlike someone I could mention." She started to turn back to her writing.

Gregg sighed. "I'm sorry." He ran his hand through his hair in a gesture that brought a knot to Anna's throat. That had been his father's way of expressing frustration or helplessness, or both. As a child, she knew how to comfort him, reassure him. But he'd long since outgrown his need for her. Or had he?

Anna looked at Gregg then settled back in her chair. "Karen's a lovely girl, Gregg. I'm already fond of her. I don't know why she's here, and I don't expect you to tell me. But I do know something upset her. She has very expressive eyes, very vulnerable eyes. If you're using her for some reason, think twice about it. She's falling in love with you."

Gregg stared at her, his laugh bitter. He shoved his hands into the pockets of his jeans. "Not likely! She considers me something more suited to living under a rock—or at least in a cave. I'm afraid Ms. McGraw's only interest in me is as a lead to a juicy story."

"You can't believe that!" Anna said, shocked.

"Don't I? I've seen her in action before."

"So have I. When we lost Rock. I reread her article last night."

"She told you about that?" Gregg's voice sounded surprised.

"What do you mean, told me? I remembered the name of the writer. McGraw. I checked again and the initials K. D. were good enough for me. I knew the writer was a young girl, which Karen would have been at the time."

"She wrote it," Gregg admitted reluctantly.

"So what's the problem?" Anna asked.

Gregg turned toward the window. "We've had a few clashes before. I needed her help on this case, so we called a truce."

"So you're using her," Anna said, her voice flat.

Gregg's jaw clenched. "No more than she's using me."

Anna turned back to her writing. "Don't be so sure of that."

Gregg tapped on Karen's door. Tapped again. When he received no answer he turned the knob and peeked inside. He drew in his breath when he saw her on the bed. Unable to resist, he crossed the room to look down at her. She was lying on her side, completely swathed in the cotton throw. Her damp hair tumbled around her head, partly covering her face.

Gregg clenched his fists. He wanted to touch her, feel her softness, her warmth. Why not? He asked himself now. She was asleep. Very carefully, he

55

sat on the edge of the bed and reached out to brush the hair from her face.

Karen stirred and Gregg held his breath. She turned onto her back. Her thigh now pressed tightly against his and Gregg feared that if he moved she would awaken.

She moaned and moved her head restlessly. Her lips parted and as Gregg stared at their luscious fullness, he became aware that her eyes had opened and she was looking at him in confusion.

"Gregg?" She sat up. "Is something wrong?" She touched his arm.

He shook his head, not sure he could trust his voice. "If you want to get dressed," he managed after a moment, "I thought you might like to go for a ride in the boat."

"What time is it?" she asked, her voice still slurred with sleep.

"Five. We still have a couple of hours before dinner."

She lay back, stretching luxuriously. "I guess I should get up if I want to sleep tonight."

"I'm sorry you didn't sleep last night," Gregg said, not looking at her.

He felt her glance. "Did you?" she asked.

He looked at her then and she read the answer in the shadows under his eyes. She rose to a sitting position again.

"It's almost over," she said gently.

"But the hardest part is still ahead."

She nodded, swallowed. "Notifying the family." She hesitated. "Can I—I'd like to be there—if it would help," she said, her voice uncertain.

His mouth tightened. "We can talk about it later."

She sighed. "I'll get dressed."

Eva O'Connor

He stood. "Come down to the dock when you're ready." There was no warmth or welcome in his voice, only resignation.

Karen stared after him, wondering why she would put herself at such emotional risk by spending time with him. Her mouth twisted. It didn't seem to be a conscious choice any more. She needed to be with him as much as she needed the air she breathed.

Gregg looked up as he heard footsteps on the dock. Karen came toward him with an easy confident stride, her casual shoes and windbreaker perfect attire for a boat ride. His frown deepened. It would be so much easier to nurture his antagonism if he could find justification for it. The truth was, since he'd asked her to work with him, he could find no fault with anything she did. In fact, he now doubted his original assessment of her. That could prove dangerous. Sometimes all a cop had to go on was his ability to size up people. It would appear that in Karen McGraw's case, he'd been way off base all along.

Karen looked up and saw his frown and her face closed. The ache deep inside her solidified into something almost tangible. How she wanted to see him relax, to see his lips soften in a smile and his eyes sparkle with laughter.

Gregg saw the closed expression on Karen's face, the hurt in her eyes. He knew he was responsible for the change, but he didn't know what to do about it. He wanted her so much it was beginning to affect his judgment. The only thing he had left was the knowledge that she was all wrong for him.

"Permission to come aboard?" Karen stood above him on the dock.

"Permission granted." He reached up and steadied her as she stepped down. Then before he could release her, a swell caught the small craft and threw her off balance. Braced against the rocking of the boat, his arm tightened as he pulled her against him.

Karen drew in her breath as she felt herself falling, but before she had time to be afraid, she felt Gregg's arm around her, steadying, tightening, protecting. She closed her eyes as she sought to regain her equilibrium, and forced herself to step away from him.

"Thank you," she said. "I didn't mean to be so clumsy."

His glance swept the lake. "The wind is picking up. I hadn't noticed. This may get a little bumpy." He looked back and his eyes questioned her.

Karen shrugged. "Why not? It's been awhile since I've done anything on the edge."

He tossed her a life jacket. "We don't get *that* close to the edge," he said. "Find a seat and we'll get started."

She shrugged into the jacket and watched Gregg do the same. Then he bent to start the engine and moments later they were skimming across the lake.

Karen squinted through her lashes, giving herself over to the pleasure of watching the blurred scenery as it swept past and the rock solid figure of the man at the wheel. Gregg stood with legs spread. The wind molded his jacket to his body and plastered his dark hair against his head.

Karen jerked up with a start. How long had she been staring at Gregg? The scenery had disappeared and the boat was slowing, describing a wide arc in the middle of the lake before coming to a stop, bobbing on the waves. Gregg cut the engine then turned, pinning her with his gaze.

"Okay," he grated. "Let's have it. Why couldn't you sleep last night?"

Karen stared at him. She was trapped. Dead center in the middle of the lake in a boat barely big enough to hold the two of them. She had no where to go, and she had a feeling Gregg didn't plan on them going anywhere until he had the answers he wanted.

She twined her fingers together, wet her lips. "Well, first of all, you broke your promise." Her voice was so low she didn't know if Gregg could hear it above the wind. She did not meet his eyes.

He reached down and caught her chin in his hand, turned her face so he could look into it. "What promise was that?"

She closed her eyes against the burning passion in his. "You said you'd be there if this got to be too much. But last night—you just walked away!" A shudder rippled through her.

Gregg straightened, stared out over the water. "I walked away because it was too much for me, can you understand? I didn't have anything to offer you." The harshness of his voice underscored his struggle for control.

"I told you I'm here, if there's anything I can do—"

"There isn't anything you can do. I don't want you to do anything. I don't want you to help me!" He sank down on a bench and dropped his head in his hands. His voice was muffled and Karen wasn't sure she heard correctly. *"I don't want to need you!"*

Karen looked at his bent head, his fingers splayed through his hair, and a lump caught in her throat. She started to stand, to turn away, to put just a little distance between them. The boat rolled on a swell and she pitched forward. She saw the deck coming up at her, the corner of a bench, then she felt arms close around her, lifting her.

"Karen!" Gregg's voice was a helpless groan as he folded her in his arms. "I'm sorry I wasn't strong enough last night. I wanted to comfort you. I knew you needed me. I was afraid—" His lashes fell, swept up as his eyes met hers. "I was afraid I couldn't walk away."

She pulled away from him. "I understand," she said, deliberately keeping her voice casual.

"You do?" He seemed surprised, and more than a little suspicious.

"I understand how important it is that you be able to walk away when this is over." She raised her head to meet his gaze fully.

Gregg stared at her. "That's what you want, too. Isn't it?" His harsh voice demanded an answer.

Karen made her way to a seat. "I want to go back now. You were right. It's gotten a little bumpy."

He glared at her then bent to start the engine. They shot forward, recklessly this time. She could judge the extent of Gregg's anger by the way he handled the boat. She supposed she should have been frightened, but her need for him was so raw, so elemental, she felt at one with the wind that stung her face and tore at her hair.

CHAPTER SIX

Back at the dock Gregg secured the boat. He jumped onto the landing and held a hand down to Karen. She laughed as she scrambled up beside him.

"Well, that was fun!" she said, her eyes sparkling, her hair a tangled mass of curls. "Maybe we can do it again sometime!"

She knew she was pushing him, felt also that he would never lose control. As she made to brush past him, his hand shot out to close around her arm. He pulled her back against him, his arm a steel band crushing the breath from her.

"Gregg!" Her voice was a small whimper of fear as she stared into the violence of his eyes.

"Let's see how much you enjoy this?" His voice rasped across her fragile emotions and she cringed as she saw his mouth descend toward hers.

She struggled and his arms tightened. Then his lips were on hers, hard, punishing, demanding. Softening, seeking, giving.

Karen sagged against Gregg, her arms clasped around his neck. If he loosened his hold on her, she knew she would fall. He reached up to free her hands, holding them in his. He looked into her face and she let him see everything—hiding nothing that she felt.

Gregg drew a ragged breath as he read her need, her vulnerability. Her lips were swollen from his ravishment and her eyelids drooped seductively. She rested against him, emotionally drained, and he knew she wanted more. He ground his teeth. He did, too. His mouth tightened and he released her, turning away to throw a cover over the boat and fasten it.

Karen wrapped her arms around herself, the wind suddenly cold and biting. She felt a drop of rain.

Gregg jumped up beside her. "Come on," he shouted above the wind. "A storm is coming. We need to get back to the house." He caught her hand and half dragged her off the landing, hurrying her toward shelter.

There was no opportunity to say more. Not that she could think of anything coherent, Karen realized as she hurried along. Huge raindrops began splattering around them and she struggled to keep her pace, trying not to favor her left leg, until finally they reached the house.

He stood below her on the steps, his chest heaving as he caught his breath. Then the world outside disappeared in a solid sheet of water and he stepped up beside her, pulling her back out of reach of the blowing rain.

Karen turned back from the shelter of the porch and looked at the storm raging around them. She drew a deep calming breath. "I love storms," she said. "Even thunder and lightning." This as a brilliant flash split the sky.

Gregg looked at her for a moment, his eyes hooded. "I used to," he said. "I doubt that I ever will again." He turned and walked into the house without a backward look.

Karen stared after him, wondering that her most innocent remarks always seemed to misfire. Then she followed him and immediately understood.

Kelly, sobbing hysterically, threw herself into Gregg's arms. He folded her close, his head bent over hers as he murmured words of comfort. Kyle stood beside them, his hand stroking her arm, his eyes anxious. Anna, seeing Karen, pulled herself away from the group and wiped her eyes.

"She's been like this ever since her mother was killed," Anna explained. "Megan lost control of her car in a storm. I know Kelly still has nightmares, and when it storms, she goes into hysterics."

So much for her brilliant remark about loving storms, Karen thought as lightning flashed again. She was already moving toward the window. "We need to close the drapes," she told Anna. "To shut out the lightning flashes and as much of the sound as possible. Can you put on some music? Whatever Kelly likes to relax—the louder, the better."

Anna looked at her for a moment as comprehension dawned. She smiled. "Why didn't I think of that? It sounds as if it might help. It certainly can't hurt."

Karen busied herself closing blinds in the kitchen and continued through the house. The sound of the storm was much less in the den, she noted. If she could get Gregg to bring Kelly in here, it would be even better. Anna was in a corner, searching through a collection of CD's.

"I really don't know much about these things," Anna said.

Karen took the CD from her. "I'll take care of it. See if you can get Kelly in here. Notice how much quieter it is." She inserted the CD and turned up the volume, aware that Anna had hurried from the room. A moment later she heard voices, and decided she shouldn't be intruding on such private sorrow. She slipped from the room as Gregg and Kelly entered.

Midnight had come and gone. The storm rumbled in the distance and faded away. Karen stood on the balcony looking out at a world washed clean and drenched in moonlight.

Dinner had been a strain. Kelly picked at her food and everyone seemed tense and edgy. Kyle and Anna tried to draw Karen into the conversation, but she was too concerned about Kelly and too aware of Gregg to be herself. Almost immediately after dinner, Anna took Kelly upstairs to tuck her into bed and Karen excused herself.

Now, having missed the storm, she sought to enjoy the calm that should follow. A jagged sigh tore through her. *Whatever madness had possessed her to spend the weekend here?* She felt as if she'd never know peace again.

She jumped as the door behind her slid open and Gregg stepped out. The balcony felt as small as the boat. His presence crowded out everything else. She made a small movement away from him.

Gregg froze and his voice sounded strained as it came out of the darkness. "Are you afraid of me?"

She searched his face, shadowed in the moonlight. She swallowed. "Should I be?"

He moved to the railing and leaned his arms on it. He looked toward the lake, calm and glassy now. "I don't know. I don't know what you want."

Karen decided not to pursue that subject. "How is Kelly?" she asked.

She felt his glance. "Better than expected. However you knew what to do, it worked. We usually have to sedate her."

Karen stared at him. "This has been going on for three years?"

He nodded. "She was only sixteen. I wasn't much help." He turned away. "I couldn't believe Megan was gone, either. Not after losing Rock the way we did." He raked a hand through his hair. "We all have our hang ups. Kyle's a little too reckless, believing that if life is all that short, he may as well enjoy it to the max."

"And you?" Karen asked when he didn't continue. "I don't suppose you have any hang ups you'd care to talk about?"

"None I'd care to talk about," Gregg agreed. "But I'm afraid you know about them all the same."

Karen shook her head. "Not really. I haven't been able to see anything beneath the hard-boiled facade and the cynicism." Her mouth twisted.

"Not much you haven't!" He sounded angry.

Karen turned to look at him. "What do you mean?"

"For one thing, you have to know how much I want you."

She shook her head, her throat tight. "I only know how much you resent me—dislike me." Her hands tightened on the railing. "I had a wonderful time today, but I shouldn't have come. I hope you don't think you have to ask me back."

"I don't want you to feel that way." His voice grew husky, his hands on her arms as he turned her to face him. "What can I do to change your mind?"

She shook her head. "I've mastered the art of self-preservation."

"Self-preservation is an instinct." Gregg's mouth was inches from hers.

"Then it has served me well in the past." She forced herself to breathe.

"What does it tell you to do now?" he asked, drawing her closer.

She turned her face away. "To run. To hide. To escape at all costs."

"And where will you run?" His fingers were on her chin, turning her face to his.

"Please, Gregg—"

"Please, what?"

"Please, don't!"

His breath rasped harshly. "I have to!" he groaned. He drew her close, his embrace infinitely tender as his mouth found hers.

"Gregg—"

"Kiss me!" he said.

Because she wanted this more than life, Karen raised her face to his, twined her arms around his neck. For a moment her mouth clung to his.

Then she lowered her arms and pulled away. "I can't do this!" she whispered, her eyes dark and troubled. "As much as I want to—" She broke off as she realized what she'd admitted. She turned away to lean her elbows on the railing, her face in her hands. Her breath came in shallow gasps.

Gregg's arms slipped around her and he nuzzled his face in her hair. "It's enough that you want to," he said with teasing gentleness.

She shook her head as if he hadn't spoken. "I don't do casual affairs, Gregg. There are too many reasons not to, and they don't work for me."

He turned her around. "What makes you think I'd be interested in a casual affair?" His voice had hardened.

"I think you'd run a hundred miles in the other direction if you thought it was anything more."

His hands tightened on her arms. "And you just called me a hard-boiled cynic or something to that effect. I guess you'd know." He released her and turned away. "Do you think there's anything more?"

Karen wet her lips. "Do I think there's anything more than what?"

She heard him mutter something under his breath. "Do you think there's anything more here than a casual affair?"

"For you or for me?"

He swung around. "You think there's a difference?"

"I'm sure of it." She was trembling, but she kept her voice even.

"In other words, we couldn't possibly want the same things from life?"

"I believe that accurately parallels the differences you drew between cops and reporters in the park a week ago when this all started."

"A lot can happen in a week." His voice was barely audible.

"I know," she whispered, too low for him to hear.

Gregg gave a sigh of resignation and straightened. "Kelly and Kyle are leaving in the morning to drive back to school. I want to leave around one."

Karen nodded. "I'll be ready."

Gregg turned and slid the door open. "Try to get some sleep." He stepped through the door and it closed with a click of finality.

Karen waited in the den as Kelly and Kyle got ready to leave. She glanced at the pictures on the walls, not really seeing them, vaguely aware of the voices just outside.

A picture above the mantle caught her attention and she knew with absolute certainty that it was Gregory McClaren, clan patriarch. She could see a resemblance to the present Gregg, especially in the eyes. Gregory appeared to have been of much slighter build and had light brown, almost red hair.

In smaller groupings followed the succeeding generations of McClarens. With a reporter's eye for detail, Karen quickly spotted resemblances and traced the family tree through the generations. Then she stopped, a frown creasing her brow.

"That's Gregg and Megan when they were nineteen, just before she married Rock. He's the--"

"Yes. I recognized him." Karen tore her eyes from the photo and turned to Anna who had silently entered the room. "In all the times he's mentioned Megan, Gregg never told me they were twins, too." She shook her head. "No wonder he's had so much trouble since losing her."

"It wasn't just losing her. He and Rock were best friends." Anna shook her head a little at the remembrance. "When Rock and Megan married I worried a little about Gregg's relationship with him, but it only seemed to grow stronger. Then, the next year, right after Kelly and Kyle were born, I lost my husband—Gregg's father. He and Rock pitched in and saved the ranch. When we lost Rock, I didn't know which one to worry about the most, Megan or Gregg."

"I went to Rock's funeral, but I never got a good look at Megan because she wore a veil. I never knew they were twins. That explains a lot."

"Is that how you and Gregg met, at Rock's funeral?" Anna asked.

"Not really. We ran into each other several years later and he made it clear that he didn't care much for reporters. In all our succeeding clashes, he only wants to attribute me with the most mercenary and self-serving motives." She stood, moved to a window. "Who knows? Maybe he's right." She sounded defeated. "This case was a test. '*A chance to change my image,*' he said."

"That's not why you took it," Anna said with certainty.

Karen looked at her, shook her head. "No. It isn't."

"You've told me how my son feels about you," Anna said. "Would it be asking too much to ask how you feel about him?"

"It would," Karen said without hesitation. "Particularly since I haven't figured it out myself. Please excuse me."

Anna held her gaze for a moment, nodded. "Of course."

Karen stepped out of the den into the middle of a discussion between Kyle and Gregg. She drew back out of sight.

"But next weekend is Easter," Kyle was saying. "We get a long weekend. We thought we'd like one last ski trip before the season ends."

"I understand that." Gregg's voice was even, reasonable. "But you don't have enough experience to fly in the mountains. The weather is too unpredictable, the winds—"

"Then come with us," Kelly moved up beside her brother. "You can fly the plane."

"Sure," Kyle said smoothly. "Bring Karen. The cabin is big enough for all of us. Gram has other plans. She won't miss us."

"Karen probably has plans," Gregg said. Karen thought she heard a thread of anger in his voice. Obviously, he didn't want her along.

"Have you asked her?" Kelly asked. "She doesn't have any family—"

Karen slipped back into the den and out the side door. She didn't see Anna turn from the corner and look after her anxiously.

Karen managed her good-bys to Kelly and Kyle, avoiding Gregg in the process. Kelly looked rested, she thought with relief. A little pale, but much better than last night.

She hugged them both. "Be careful driving," she said. "By the way, why aren't you flying back? The weather seems perfect."

"Gregg thinks he may need the plane for a couple of days," Kyle said. "Some business trip." He looked at her. "You don't know about it? I assumed you were going with him. In fact, that's why he wants the plane."

"Maybe he forgot to mention it," Karen shrugged. "Take care!" She waved and turned back into the house, bumping into Gregg as he came out to say his good-bys.

He caught her arms to steady her, searched her face. "I need to talk to you," he said. "Wait here. I won't be a moment."

Her arms going around herself instinctively, she wandered into the den. Anna had opened the windows to air the house.

"It always smells so fresh and wonderful after a storm," Anna smiled. "I like to open everything and bring it inside for awhile."

Karen tried to smile, but apparently it wasn't a very good attempt. Anna straightened, looking at Karen.

"Karen, Kelly told me about your mother this morning. I'm so sorry. I knew her." Anna's voice was gentle, sympathetic.

Karen's head jerked up. "You knew her?"

"Well, actually, I knew your father better. But when he married Beth, we became friends—until they moved."

"I didn't even know my father," Karen said in disbelief. "It seems incredible for someone else to say they knew him."

"Jason McGraw was one of the finest men I've ever known," Anna said, hurt at Karen's attitude. "He died soon after you were born."

"That's the only thing I've ever been told about him," Karen turned away. "If he was so wonderful, obviously he didn't deserve my mother."

Anna stared at her, stunned. "You and your mother weren't close?"

"It's a long story." Karen reached up impatiently to brush at a tear.

"You were Jason's only heir, and he was the last McGraw." Anna looked up. "Your mother didn't manage to squander everything, did she? That isn't the problem?"

Karen laughed and Anna thought she'd never heard a sound so bitter. "Not all of it, but she may as well have."

"What does that mean?" Anna looked up to see Gregg standing in the door and made a motion for him to be silent. He moved back out of sight.

"She never wanted me to be a reporter. She never wanted me to do anything useful with my life. And she did warn me, so it wasn't a complete surprise to find that she had a clause attached to the will."

"What kind of clause?" Anna asked when Karen paused.

"That unless I give up my career and move back home to the family estate and take my place in society, I don't inherit a cent."

Anna gasped. "Surely that isn't legal. How could she be so selfish?"

Karen looked at her. "You're the one who said you knew her. Well enough to suspect she may have squandered the entire estate. Me, I hardly knew her at all. I was always away at boarding school." Karen turned away. "Tell Gregg when he's ready to go I'll be down by the lake."

As Karen hurried from the room, Gregg stepped in. Anna looked at him. "How much did you hear?" she asked, her voice full of concern.

"Most of it." He caught her hands. "Should I go after her? Try and talk to her?"

"I don't know." Anna searched his face, a mixture of love and

71

disappointment in her eyes. "Do you plan to hurt her even more than she's already been hurt?"

"How can I hurt her?" Gregg asked impatiently.

"I guessed that she was in love with you from the first. Now I'm even more convinced. But she thinks you feel nothing for her but contempt."

"I know," Gregg said. "I got that message last night."

"So what are you going to do about it?" Anna asked.

He looked at her for a moment then grinned. "Does being my mother give you the right to be so nosy?" he teased.

"You'd better believe it! She doesn't know it, but Karen is very much like her father. Start over, dear. Give yourself a chance to know her."

He shook his head. "I don't need to start over. I already know what I need to know about her. But there's so much history, so many bad feelings to overcome, I'm not sure she'll give me a chance."

CHAPTER SEVEN

Karen sat on a branch overhanging the lake, her feet dangling in the water. Gregg watched for a moment before speaking, afraid of startling her.

"That might not be a good idea," he said.

Karen looked up. "What's not a good idea?"

"Putting your feet in the water." He knelt on the bank and pulled a blade of grass to chew on. "We've been known to have snakes."

She didn't shriek or flinch or jerk her feet out of the water as he expected. Instead, she looked at him steadily. "It's still too cold for snakes," she said as a statement of fact.

He shot to his feet. "Then why do you have your feet in the water?"

She sighed and pulled them up. She walked back along the limb to jump onto the bank. Gregg caught her and lifted her down.

"It was a distraction while it lasted," she said.

His eyes filled with laughter. "Is that the same philosophy as walking over hot coals? Only you turn your feet into blocks of ice?"

"Probably." She did not share his amusement, but looked around. "My shoes should be here somewhere."

He picked them up from the rock where she had placed them. "And your socks," he said, handing them to her. "Your feet are still wet."

"I'll walk back barefoot—" she began.

"Not on your life," he said. "You might hurt yourself."

She stared at him. "How?"

"You might step on something, cut yourself—"

She made a sound of dismissal and turned away.

Gregg reached her in two steps and swung her up into his arms. "If you insist on going back now, I'll carry you."

"No, Gregg, please, put me down!" Her voice was pleading, desperate in its seriousness. He lowered her to her feet, but did not release her.

"You are afraid of me!" he whispered in disbelief.

She couldn't meet his eyes. "Not of you."

"Then what?" He caught her chin, tried to look into her face. She closed her eyes. "What are you afraid of, Karen?" he insisted.

She sighed, a tremulous sigh that shook her body. "I'm afraid of what you make me feel. I've never been close to anyone, and I know I'm the last person you want to be close to." The words tumbled over one another. "I

74

don't think we should work together anymore. The case is all but solved. You can identify the kids now. I've always been a loner. I need space."

"Is that what you want?" Gregg asked. "Never to see me again."

"It's best—for both of us—"

"Liar!"

She looked up and caught her breath. His mouth curved up, his eyes sparkled with laughter.

"Oh, Gregg." She reached up to touch his lips. "Why did you have to do that?"

His fingers closed around hers. "What have I done?"

"Smile like that. Don't you know how hard you are to resist—even when you're glaring at me?"

He kissed her fingers. "I'll never glare at you again."

"You will. Nothing I stand for could ever please you."

"Karen—" He sighed, a sigh of frustration that came from deep inside. "It seems I'm the one who needs to change his image. Is there any way you could bring yourself to believe me if I say that I've misjudged you at every turn, that I've never given you a chance? Can we start over—"

She stared at him, a nagging fear at the back of her mind, something she didn't want to face. She turned away, brought her hands up to put them over her ears. After a moment she turned back to look at him, her face closed.

"You were right behind me. You said you wouldn't be a moment. Did you overhear the conversation I had with your mother immediately after I bumped into you?"

Gregg felt his heart sink. If he wanted more from this than a casual relationship—if he wanted anything at all—he couldn't start by lying to her.

"I heard."

"So." Karen twisted her hands together.. "That explains a lot."

"Such as?"

"Karen McGraw, the reporter, is a pain in the neck, as far as you're concerned. She's everything you hate—"

"That isn't true," Gregg tried to protest.

"But Karen McGraw, the heiress, especially if she's forced to give up her career as a reporter in order to collect said fortune, might be worth your while—whatever compromises that might entail."

His stare was incredulous. "How can you even think that?"

"Perhaps the same way you can think that all reporters are scheming, shallow, conniving, and mercenary—and whatever else you've thought over the years." She sat down on a rock and began pulling on her socks and shoes, all her feelings mercifully on hold. She stood up.

"For what it's worth, I have no intention of giving up my career. I never knew my father, and my mother—" A shrug. "I've always been alone and I can manage quite well without whatever they left me." She turned to him. "So, if that's the extent of your interest, you just struck out!" She turned and walked toward the house.

Gregg started to follow Karen and stopped, raking a hand through his hair. He deserved what she thought of him, after all the times he'd hurt and misjudged her. He glanced at his watch. Eleven thirty. He had time. He turned toward the landing where the speed boat rocked gently in its berth.

Halfway to the house, Karen jerked around at the sound of the boat's engine starting. She stood motionless, a hand fluttering to her throat. She had seen Gregg in action yesterday. His recklessness knew no bounds when he was angry. Without stopping to think, she turned and hurried toward the dock.

Dear Father, keep Gregg safe. I know I pushed him too far. Please forgive me.

Slowly, engine cut back to idle, Gregg eased the boat into its berth. So intense was his concentration that he did not see Karen until he jumped onto the landing. She sat on the rough flooring, her knees drawn up, her arms wrapped around them. Her hair had almost straggled free of a loose ponytail. She looked as young as Kelly, and every bit as vulnerable. He wanted to reach for her, pull her into his arms, but he forced himself to go slow.

"I didn't expect to see you here," he said.

She stood with a lithe, graceful movement. "I was worried about you." She didn't look at him, but out over the lake.

"Why?" He bent to tie the boat then busied himself covering it.

"That recklessness you're so worried about in Kyle," she said. "I think maybe it's inherited."

He straightened with an easy grin. "Point taken," he agreed. "There usually isn't anyone around to be concerned. I told you this is my escape—the way I let go."

Karen looked at him, the relaxed stance, the tousled hair, and especially his smile. She swallowed. "It seems to work," she admitted.

He laughed, put an arm around her shoulder. "Let's get started. I told Mom we'd have lunch on the way."

Karen sat curled in a corner of the seat of Gregg's truck. An unspoken truce existed between them, and she felt reluctant to break it with conversation.

She forced herself to relax and enjoy the scenery. That wasn't hard to do. The Colorado foothills had long ago captured her heart, so different from the flat monotony of her native Kansas.

"Are you hungry?" Gregg asked about an hour later.

"Not particularly. I had a late breakfast."

"Good. I thought we could eat in Fort Morgan. A friend of mine owns a restaurant there."

"What kind of restaurant?"

"A little steak house. Very casual, if that concerns you."

"Actually, it does." She pushed her hair back.

He grinned. "You'll do fine. Just take that ridiculous ribbon out of your hair."

"What ridiculous ribbon?" She glared at him. "I'll have you know, this is a very expensive ribbon, with gold threads—"

He reached over and plucked it from her hair and dropped it into her lap. "I don't care if it is silver plated. It can't compete with your hair."

At a loss for words, Karen picked up the bright strip of fabric and smoothed it between her fingers. "My mother gave this ribbon to me. I would never have chosen it myself."

Gregg glanced at her. "Tell me about your childhood, Karen. You don't seem to have an abundance of happy memories."

"I met my grandmother once. That's probably the happiest memory I have. She and mother had a terrible fight. She wanted to take me away and let me live with her. I used to pray that would happen. And I liked my stepfather. We had common tastes."

"And those were?"

"He apparently didn't much like living with my mother, either. Fortunately for him, he had a choice. I didn't."

"What happened to him?"

"He left just before my twelfth birthday. He took my sisters with him. My mother didn't put up any fight at all. She had more than she wanted in me."

"Why didn't she let him take you? Or did he want you?"

"I think he would have. I know I wanted to go. But she had to hang onto the McGraw heiress. My mother didn't get any of my father's fortune directly. She played a caretaker role. She could use the money necessary for my upbringing and the lifestyle expected of someone in such a position. And did she ever use it. Even though she never wanted me, without me she had nothing. With me, she had access to a fortune."

"It seems your stepfather had a good thing going. Why didn't he stick with her?"

"This may be hard for someone like you to understand," Karen said, "but not everyone is willing to ransom their soul for money. I've known for at least ten years that if I pursued a life of my own, I would end up with nothing. But the trade off was my freedom. I couldn't pay the price. For almost twenty years, I forced myself to live the life she chose for me, did my best to please her. For the last ten, I've lived my own. My stepfather made the same choice. As much as I missed him and my sisters, I fully understood his reasoning."

"Is he still alive?"

"Yes."

"Did he attend your mother's funeral?"

"Of course. She did give birth to his children."

"Do they inherit anything?"

"No. Not unless I choose to share. And since I won't collect, I don't have that choice."

"Hmmm."

Karen glanced at him. "That '*hmmm*' has a note of censorship in it."

"Just thinking." His voice remained conversational. "Is selfishness another trait that can be inherited?"

"No doubt," Karen replied. "Believe it or not, I've considered that possibility."

"And it doesn't bother you? Your career is that important?"

She shifted in her seat. "You know, of all people, I should think you'd understand."

"Why would I, in particular, understand?"

"You work as a police officer."

"I do, I'm proud to say."

"Why?"

"Why?" He shot her a glance. "Because it needs to be done."

"And?"

"And I happen to be good at what I do."

"Do you enjoy it?"

"Not all of it, no."

"And you certainly don't do it for money or prestige."

"Your point, exactly?"

She sighed. "Gregg, I've seen your Eden. We left it a few miles back, remember? You belong there. You have everything anyone could want—"

"Have you ever heard of trying to make things a little better for those who don't happen to have as much as you?"

"My point, exactly," Karen said softly.

She saw his jaw tighten as he considered this. "And all that applies to you as well?" he asked after a moment. "You think your career somehow serves your fellow man?"

Karen could not stop her harshly indrawn breath at his words. She pressed her lips together and closed her eyes. "No, if you put it that way, I guess not. My career is totally frivolous." She looked at him. "If I ask a question, will you give me an honest answer?"

"Why would I lie?"

"Okay. Have you ever read anything I've written?"

"No. I generally don't have much time for reading outside of work related material."

"Not even the article on Rock?"

"I didn't need to read that. I knew who he was."

"I see." She settled back in the seat. "Forget lunch. I think I'd rather just get home." She picked up the ribbon and tied her hair back with fingers that trembled slightly.

Karen climbed the steps to her apartment and stopped abruptly. Barricade tape that read 'Police Crime Scene' ran back and forth across the bashed in door. She put a hand to her mouth and reached out to catch the railing for support.

"My dear!" Karen looked up to see the manager of the apartment complex hurrying up the stairs. "I saw your car and I wanted to warn you."

She put an arm around Karen's shoulder and led her back down the stairs and into her office. "I called the police as soon as your neighbor reported that your door had been kicked in. They suspect it's just random violence. It looks as if everything is pretty much destroyed. Fortunately you still have most everything in storage."

Karen could only stare at her, dazed.

"I tried to find you another apartment, but everything we have is either full or being redecorated. You're welcome to stay with me for a couple of nights—"

Karen shook her head. "Thank you," she managed in a hoarse whisper, "but I'll manage. May I use your phone?"

Gregg turned into the driveway of his rented duplex and cut the engine. He sat for a moment, wishing for some way to vent his frustration. Back at the ranch, he would go out in the boat. It had worked this morning, short lived though it had turned out to be. He sighed. Maybe a long run.

Why was he so tough on Karen? Why did he always cut her down and belittle her job? He hated himself when he saw the hurt look in her eyes, but he couldn't seem to stop himself from saying cruel, thoughtless things to her.

With a sigh he got out of the truck and unlocked the door. He glanced at his answering machine to see a flashing light indicating several messages. He dropped his duffel bag and punched the button. As the first message began to play he went through to the kitchen.

Gregg returned to hear the end of a message. ". . .knew you were working with her so thought you'd like to know." He recognized the voice of an officer who had weekend duty. With a frown he pressed the rewind button and waited impatiently for the message to replay.

"Gregg, this is Jack. Karen McGraw's apartment was vandalized early this morning. We don't know if it was a random act, or an act of vengeance. She's been involved in some pretty serious *exposes'* lately, and called a few weeks ago to say she'd received threats. Anyway, I knew you were working with her so thought you'd like to know."

CHAPTER SEVEN

Gregg ran up the stairs to Karen's apartment and stopped at the barricade tape. He'd seen her car in the parking lot. *Where could she be?* He raced down the stairs and headed for the manager's office.

Dear God, please let Karen be safe. Please help me take care of her.

Gregg saw Karen through the window and slowed his steps long enough to catch his breath before pushing open the door. She was talking on the phone and didn't look up.

"What do you mean, you have nothing available?" Her voice sounded hoarse. "Yes, I've heard. There's a convention in town." She replaced the receiver with a heartfelt sigh, glanced up and saw Gregg. Her face registered nothing, as if she had no emotion left.

"Why didn't you call me when you saw what had happened?" he asked.

"Why would I? The police have already been here. I'm to go down in the morning and fill out a report, in case I might know something that would help. Meantime, I have no clothing and no place to stay. Unless—" Something occurred to her and she picked up the phone again and began dialing.

"Who are you calling now?"

"Comforting Arms," she replied evenly.

He stared at her. "That's a shelter for battered and abandoned women!"

"So? Right now I can't think of anyone more alone than I am." Her lips trembled before she pressed them together.

Gregg reached over and depressed the switch hook.

For the first time since he'd arrived, he saw emotion on Karen's face. Pure unadulterated anger blazed in her eyes.

"Why did you do that?" she asked. She began redialing the number.

He took the receiver and replaced it. "You're coming with me."

"Not likely!"

"We can do this one of two ways. You either come with me willingly, or I take you into protective custody."

"On what grounds?" Karen challenged.

"Jack thinks this may have been an act of vengeance. I'd like to hear your feelings on the subject."

"*My feelings on the subject?* Obviously, everything I write is so trivial, how could it possibly upset anyone?" She held his eyes as anger simmered in hers.

She had the satisfaction of seeing a dark flush creep up his neck and his own eyes sparked with anger.

"Are you going to tell me what you've been working on?" he asked.

"For the past week I've been helping you—"

A muscle in his jaw tightened. "Karen—" he warned.

"They have really good archives at the *Clarion*. They even know who I am down there. I—"

"I admit I deserve your contempt," Gregg said. "But right now I don't have time for this. Your life may be in danger. I need to know what's going on if I'm to do anything about it."

"Who asked you to do anything about it?" she replied. "Mrs. Morgan said the police suspect random violence. I'm willing to accept that."

"As I said, the message Jack left suggested it might be an act of vengeance. He said you called a few weeks ago. Said you'd received threats."

"I'll bet he wrote all the details down in the police report," Karen said. "He probably even has it filed under my name."

Gregg sighed. "I'm afraid you leave me no choice."

Her eyes widened in question.

"I'm taking you into custody."

"What makes you think I need your protection?" she asked. "Before I ran into you a week ago, I had been able to manage my life all right."

"And tonight?" he asked. "No apartment, no hotel rooms available. Where do you plan to stay?"

"I tried to call Comforting Arms," she reminded with infinite patience.

"That's not an option," he grated.

"It's a perfectly viable option—" Karen began.

The door opened and the manager bustled in. She looked from Gregg to Karen and back to Gregg. She smiled.

"Officer Watson!" she greeted. "How nice to see you!"

Karen rolled her eyes as Gregg turned to Mrs. Morgan, all charm now.

Mrs. Morgan turned back to Karen. "I'm sorry, my dear," she said, remembering her mission. "The apartment hasn't been vacated yet. I'm afraid I have nothing to offer you—except as I said—"

"That's perfectly all right," Gregg broke in. "I just heard and I came over to get her. She has a place to stay."

"That's wonderful!" Mrs. Morgan gushed. "I'm so relieved, my dear. I've worried about you all day. Now I know you're in good hands."

"Thanks, Mrs. Morgan." Karen gave her a quick hug. "I'll call tomorrow and give you a number. Let me know as soon as you have an apartment ready."

"Of course."

Karen let Gregg lead her out of the office and out to the parking lot. As soon as they were out of sight of Mrs. Morgan, she pulled away from him and headed for her car.

He hurried after her and matched his stride to hers. "And may I ask where you think you're going?"

She unlocked the car and threw her bag inside. "I'm heading east. In a hundred miles or so, I'll stop and find a hotel for the night. Tomorrow I'll go home and claim my inheritance. After I've given it all away, I don't suppose there's anything in my mother's will that would prevent me from going somewhere else and starting over."

Gregg caught her arm, looked into her face. "You're serious," he said. "Karen, you can't do this."

"Exactly what am I doing that you don't approve?" she asked, her mouth twisting.

"For one thing, you're bailing out on me in the middle of a job."

"One where you no longer want me along," she said. "You don't have to put things in writing for me, Gregg. I'm fairly sharp. I got your message."

"Then I apologize. I want you along. I need you along." His voice was low, persuasive. It was almost possible to believe he meant the words he spoke.

Karen shook her head. "What kind of fool do you think I am that I'd hang around after the things you've said to me? You belittle me as a human being. You mock my work—"

"I'm sorry."

"I know I've made mistakes, but they weren't deliberate or intentional. I never meant to hurt anyone. I really don't know why you hate me so much." She started to get into the car. "All I know is that I can't handle it anymore. Maybe my mother had my best interests at heart after all. There's no longer any thing here that I want, or have any hope of getting." She looked at Gregg for a moment with unconscious longing. Then, with an abrupt movement, she turned back to the car.

"Karen!" He caught her arm and pulled her around to face him.

She pulled her arm free and turned away from his burning gaze. "Let me go, Gregg!"

"I can't."

"Of course you can. Just step aside."

He reached out to touch her face, to trace his knuckles down the silken smoothness of her cheek. "It's been too late for me to step aside since I found you crying beside the crosses in the park. Crying for kids you didn't even know. Do you know that I had just got through asking God for help on the case? It took a while to realize He sent you. Then after I held you, I had to think of some way to keep you near me. I knew all my antagonism had melted away, but I hoped you didn't know. I—please say something," he said, suddenly charmingly vulnerable.

Karen wet her lips. "Why?"

"You've already figured out how hard it was for me to lose Rock and Megan, and my father, too, a few years ago. At each of those times in my life, I had been involved with someone. Someone I thought seriously about a future with. And each time, when things got tough, they disappeared.

"After my father's death, I spent too much time on the ranch. I didn't have time to spend with anyone. After Rock died, and I brought Megan and the twins back to the ranch, no one wanted a ready made family. Then after Megan died, no one wanted to be an instant mother to two teenagers. I—it's been a little hard to trust anyone, their motives, their intentions. But there's been something between us from the first moment you looked up and glared into my eyes—"

Karen looked at him. "You felt it, too?"

He brushed his thumb across her lips, felt them quiver. "I felt it, too."

Karen trembled and turned away from him, arms clasped across her chest. "Why do I feel more threatened now than I did when I knew for certain you hated me?"

"I feel pretty exposed myself."

"So why tell me?" Her strained voice wavered on the edge of breaking.

"Because I'm about to lose you. You plan to walk out of my life. I can't let you do that without telling you how I feel."

"And how long will you want me around this time? Oh, I know we have to see this through. We have to get a positive identification on Matt and Juliana and notify their family. Maybe even attend a funeral."

She looked at him. "And then I'm going to close down Dr. Fumara. I know you aren't going to like that, but I don't particularly care. My job is important—maybe not as important as yours, but important still. I've done a lot of good in the past."

Dear God, please let Gregg understand how important this is. Why I have to do it.

She shook her head. "It won't work, Gregg. There's an inherent conflict here and you can't see around it. I have a lot of respect for you and what you do, but that respect isn't mutual. I don't know you. You won't allow me to. Please let me go. I can't play this game any longer."

"I can't," he repeated.

She sighed in defeat. "I'll follow you in my car."

He raised his brows. "No."

"You don't trust me—"

"It isn't that. You're leaving your car here. I've already asked for a twenty-four hour watch on it. If someone attempts to touch it, we'll know the attack on your apartment wasn't random."

"You don't have that kind of manpower," Karen protested. "And what you do have could certainly be better used elsewhere."

"If it makes you feel any better, we're going to set up a surveillance camera and an audible alarm. Mrs. Morgan will call if the alarm goes off."

"Can we stop by my office?" Karen asked.

Gregg frowned. "Why?"

She reached into the car and pulled out her duffel bag. She dropped it at his feet. "The only clothes I have are in here and they need to be washed. According to Mrs. Morgan, everything in my apartment was destroyed. Not that I expect you to let me go in and check. I put a lot of things in storage before I went to Kansas, not knowing how long I'd be gone, but I can't get to them tonight. I always keep a travel bag at work, packed so I can leave on a moment's notice. If I could get it tonight, at least I'd have something to wear tomorrow."

Gregg nodded. "We'll stop by your office." He looked as if he wanted to say more, then shook his head and turned away.

Karen turned the key in the door to her office and reached for the light switch. She stared in stunned horror.

"Karen!" Gregg grabbed for her as she started to go inside. He could see over her shoulder that her office, too, had been vandalized. He gently pushed her aside and went in.

"There's nothing we can do tonight," he said, looking at her in apology. "I'll get a team over here in the morning."

"How did they get in?" she asked, the reporter surfacing again. She looked back at the door. "The lock wasn't damaged."

Gregg went over and pushed aside a curtain. "The window is broken."

"You'd think someone would have heard."

"What kind of security do you have around here?"

"Not that good, obviously." Her voice was dry.

"Where do you keep your bag?" Gregg asked. "Is there any chance—"

"I have a locker. Maybe they don't know that." She went out and Gregg turned off the light. He closed the door and followed her down the hall.

A moment later she emerged from the ladies' room carrying a garment bag. "Everything looks fine." She tried to smile reassuringly and failed. When she saw that Gregg wasn't buying her act, she sighed. "I never thought Kansas would look so good," she whispered, her lips trembling.

He reached out and pulled her to him. His hand tangled in her hair as he pressed her head against his shoulder. He wondered what had happened to the ribbon she'd been wearing and decided he was glad to see it gone.

CHAPTER EIGHT

Karen poured detergent into the washer and closed the lid. She turned off the light and wandered barefoot into the kitchen. After loaning her a T-shirt and sweatpants to wear while she did her laundry, Gregg had disappeared, presumably into his half of the duplex.

The set up wasn't so bad, she reflected as she opened the refrigerator. Gregg rented the entire duplex, sometimes subleasing the half he didn't use. Right now it was vacant, and he had made it available to Karen. She hadn't known what to expect when he'd offered her a place to stay, but now she had to admit the arrangement was little short of ideal. The only areas they shared were the kitchen and laundry room.

The refrigerator contained nothing more promising than a stick of butter and a few ice cubes. She sighed and closed the door. As she prowled through the pantry, she began to regret turning down Gregg's dinner offer.

Now that the excitement was over she was starving, and no further mention had been made of food. Without a car, she didn't have a lot of options except to have a pizza delivered. With a sigh she started back to her side of the duplex when she heard a door slam.

Gregg entered the kitchen before Karen could move. She stood rooted to the floor, wearing an oversized T-shirt stuffed into baggy sweatpants that tied at the waist. His eyes flashed with amusement.

"I thought you might be hungry," he said by way of greeting.

"Hungry?" she repeated. "I was trying to raid your refrigerator."

"What stopped you?"

"I didn't find anything."

"Sorry about that. I don't spend a lot of time here." He began taking cartons out of a bag. "Do you like Chinese food?"

"Chinese? It's my favorite."

"Mine, too. Chopsticks?"

"Of course."

"Sit down," he invited. "Dig in."

"Thanks." She sank down on a bar stool. "It smells heavenly. From Lin's?"

"Where else?" Gregg dragged another stool to the bar. "Actually, I have a confession to make."

Karen looked at him. Waited.

"Kelly called to say they'd gotten back safely. I told her I needed to pick up something to eat and she said you mentioned liking Chinese food."

Karen reached for the carton of rice. "I guess I owe her one."

Gregg nodded in relief. "So where did you learn to use chopsticks? Most people don't bother."

"Lin taught me. I did a story a few years ago on the Chinese influence on American culture. Who taught you to use them?"

"We used to have an oriental gardener," Gregg said. "I always called him Mr. Sung. He taught me how to make birds out of folded paper."

"Origami," Karen said. "I have a beautiful purple swan that a lady in the nursing home made for me." Her face clouded. "Or rather, I had one—"

"Purple?" Gregg asked to distract her.

She shrugged. "She asked my favorite color. I didn't know what she had in mind."

"So purple is your favorite color?" Gregg mused.

"Most of the time."

He looked startled. "I didn't realize one could have a favorite color only part time."

"So I'm fickle."

"I didn't say that. But it is a new concept for me."

"So. Do you have a favorite color?"

He hesitated. "Most of the time."

She looked up. "Gregg! You're making fun of me."

"No. I hadn't thought about it like that. I was thinking of a sunset and all the colors. Then just before it gets dark, the last color you see—"

"—is purple."

Their eyes met and held. Gregg turned back to his food. "My other favorite color is the sun when it comes up in the morning—molten gold."

Karen paused, her chopsticks halfway to her mouth. "And mine is the yellow of daffodils in the spring."

Gregg watched as her lips parted and closed around the morsel of food. Her fingers as she manipulated the chopsticks fascinated him. He'd never known a woman who made the act of eating seem so sumptuous.

Karen became aware of his gaze on her and shifted uncomfortably. She stood up. "Would you like a glass of water?" she asked, going to a cabinet.

"Yes, thank you." Then, as she reached up to open the doors, he was on his feet. "Let me do that." He took down a couple of glasses.

Karen went back to sit down. She heard the washer stop in the next room and stood up again. "I'll be right back."

She returned from transferring her clothes to the dryer to find that Gregg had waited for her. She sipped the water.

"Do you have any plans for next weekend?" Gregg asked.

"I don't have any plans for tomorrow," Karen said deliberately.

"But next weekend is Easter. Most people make plans ahead of time."

She shrugged. "Some of the ladies at the nursing home have been making Easter Baskets for the children's home. I promised to deliver them."

"When?"

"Whenever they're finished. They won't be given out until Easter. Sometimes I dress up as the Bunny."

"You're kidding!"

"Why would I be kidding?"

"That's how you spend your Easter?"

"What other options are available to me? I do go to church."

"Come skiing with me and the twins," Gregg invited.

She should have seen it coming, Karen realized. In truth, she'd all but forgotten the conversation she'd overheard.

"I don't think so," she replied.

"Why not? They'll never forgive me if you don't come."

"All the more reason for me not to."

He frowned. "I don't follow. You don't want them to forgive me?"

"No. I don't want to be asked just to get you off the hook with them."

"Why do you want to be asked?"

Karen stood up and carried her dishes to the sink. She turned back to him. "The next time, you could at least try to make it sound as if you'd like me along. It just happens that I overheard your conversation with them this morning. I know why you're asking." She looked at the cartons of food. "Thanks for dinner. I guess I wasn't very hungry after all." She turned and walked through the laundry room and closed the door behind her.

Karen placed a slice of bread in the toaster and lowered the lever. The elements began to glow and she breathed a sigh of relief. As hard as it had been to find the bread, she had been afraid the toaster wouldn't work.

Beside her the coffeemaker clicked on and dark fragrant liquid began streaming into the pot. She smiled. *Gregg and his coffee*. She remembered the first day she went to his office. He apparently lived on the stuff.

She glanced around for a cup and found a mug on the drain board. That figured. He probably used the same one day after day. She turned the mug upright and her lips quirked with amusement at a picture of the Tazmanian Devil.

"From Kelly," Gregg said behind her. "When she was little, she called me Uncle Taz."

Karen turned to look at him and her breath caught softly. It seemed obvious he hadn't expected to find her in the kitchen. He still wore his pajamas with the shirt unbuttoned. His chest and stomach were covered with a light sprinkling of dark curls. He hadn't shaved and his tousled hair made him irresistible—and totally desirable. Her fingers curled around the mug in her hands and the feel of the cool ceramic brought her back to reality.

"Good morning," she greeted, hating the betraying huskiness in her voice. She handed the mug to him. As he stood beside her, filling it with coffee, her toast popped up and she jumped, startled.

"Good," Gregg said. "I see you found something to eat."

"Yes. It was a challenge. Would you like some?"

"No, thank you." He watched as she spread butter and honey on the thick slice of bread. "You can actually eat that first thing in the morning?"

She glanced at the mug in his hands. "You can actually drink that first thing in the morning?" She took her toast and a glass of juice and carried it to the table.

Gregg followed to sit across from her. "I'd forgotten how disgustingly cheerful you are in the morning," he commented, his glance dark and brooding.

She looked at him. "Does being a grouch have all that much to recommend it?"

He raised his cup, drank. "Probably not."

"Then why knock something until you've tried it?"

He was silent for a moment, looked up. "Will you come to Mason's Point with me?"

"Why? You decided to let me get my kicks after all?"

"I thought I apologized for that." He made a restless movement.

Karen sighed. "I'll go. I wasn't going to ask again—but I want to go. Thank you."

"We'll go by your office first and get some of the guys started on it."

"When can I see my apartment?" Karen asked.

He winced. "Are you sure you want to?"

"I know I don't want to. But I'm the only one who'll know if there are any clues. I also need to see if there's anything I can salvage. According to Mrs. Morgan, it's basically trashed." She shivered. "I guess, after my office, it'll be pretty hard to rule out vengeance?"

"And it seems pretty obvious there's a connection to something you are or have been working on." Gregg watched her face for a reaction. "I guess I have to stop by my office and get that report from Jack."

"That sounds like a good place to start," Karen agreed.

"You could save me time if you would just tell me—" Gregg began.

She shook her head. "I can't. I'm tired of not having you take me seriously. It might be a good thing for you to realize that other people do— some perhaps even enough to want to harm me."

Karen stood beside Gregg's truck outside the filling station while he talked with the attendant. She felt numb—her emotions frozen. Did she want the man to identify Matt and Juliana? If he did, the case was solved. If not, they were back to square one. The case had already taken one cruel twist. How much more could she or Gregg take? He hadn't talked much on the drive over and she could sense the strain he labored under.

The phone in Gregg's truck began ringing and Karen glanced over at him. He was still deep in conversation with the attendant.

She opened the door and picked up the phone.

"May I help you? This is Karen McGraw. I'm working with Gregg—"

"Is it possible to speak with Mr. Watson?" The very feminine voice was hesitant, uncertain.

Karen glanced at him. "He's away from the truck for the moment. I can take a message, or have him call you back."

A moment of silence, then a sigh. "Just tell him that Matt Kelso has turned up. However, his sister and her boyfriend are still missing."

Karen clutched the phone. "Miss McFeld? This is Miss McFeld, isn't it? Please hold on. I'll get Gregg—" She looked up to see him hurrying toward the truck. "Here he is now." Karen held the phone out to him, her eyes riveted to his face. "Miss McFeld," she whispered.

As Gregg took the phone and raised it to his ear, he reached out and drew Karen against him, his arm a comforting band of strength around her.

Gregg spoke quietly, briefly. Karen heard him tell Miss McFeld that someone had just identified Juliana, but confirmed that Matt was not the young man with her.

"He what? He's back? And he'll meet us at the airport. I'm deeply grateful." Gregg cleared the huskiness from his throat. "Thank you so much, Miss McFeld. We'll see you tomorrow." He broke the connection and returned the phone to the truck. Then he wrapped both arms around Karen, clinging to her for strength. She felt him tremble.

Gregg raised his head. "As bad as this sounds, I really hoped it was Matt. I wanted them to be together. I—know what it's like to lose a sister."

His eyes closed and he drew a deep breath.

Karen looked at him, saw the pain on his face. She touched his jaw and his hand came up to catch hers, to bring it to his lips. His eyes opened.

"Thanks for being here," he whispered.

"I wouldn't be anywhere else—as long as you want me here."

Gregg looked into her eyes and saw understanding and compassion and more. Something hard and cold and foreign inside him began to melt. He drew her closer and bent his head to hers.

Karen saw the kiss coming, let it happen. She wouldn't read too much into it, she told herself. So what if he was only being charitable, thanking her for being there when he needed her. She couldn't stop herself from returning his kiss with all the love that suddenly welled inside her. Then her breath caught as she realized the depth of her feelings.

Gregg put her a little away from him. "Is something wrong?" he asked, trailing the back of a finger down her cheek. His eyes were smoky and sensuous and Karen felt herself tremble at the impact of his gaze.

She shook her head. "No. Nothing's wrong. What now?"

"We go back and check out your apartment and pick up your clothes. Tomorrow we fly to Lamar where we'll meet Father McFeld and his sister. They'll drive us to Juliana's parents. If we can find out the name of her boyfriend, we will try to contact his family and get dental records—or at least a photo to bring back here."

Karen frowned, decided to voice the thought that kept recurring. "It seems a lot of kids get misplaced during spring break."

Gregg leaned back against the truck. "Unfortunately college students are at that awkward age of wanting total independence but not yet being equipped to handle it. And now spring break is becoming more and more important to high school students, which adds to the problem."

Gregg straightened and moved away from Karen. "Then you have those parents who see spring break as an opportunity to ship the kids off and take their own vacation. In Julie's case, she didn't have anyone to call when she found herself stranded. I don't know Matt's story. He apparently loaned Juliana the car and she went to meet her boyfriend. I'm sure—well, I can only hope he had no way of knowing what they were planning."

Karen swallowed. "You know, in spite of everything I believe about the abortion, the wreck might have happened anyway. We aren't going to mention anything else, are we? Just that they were killed in the crash—and that there was a fire."

Matt looked at her, relief evident on his face. "I was afraid I was going to have to argue with you about that."

"Why? Because you think I enjoy hurting people? Why would I tell them anything that might mar their memories of their daughter?" Tears filled her eyes. "I feel for Juliana more than you can ever know. She was so young, so alone. I can't judge her."

Karen reached up to wipe impatiently at her eyes. "I see no reason for anyone else to suffer any more than they have to," she went on. She looked across the street for a long moment. "But I can see that Dr. Fumara pays."

CHAPTER NINE

Karen and Gregg climbed the stairs to her apartment and stopped before the door. Gregg tensed. Karen glanced at him, and then she saw it, too. Tied to the barricade tape and fluttering in the breeze was the ribbon she'd worn in her hair the day before.

Gregg reached out to touch it. "You were wearing this in the truck before I dropped you off at your car. I don't believe you had it on in the manager's office here. I know you didn't have it when we were at your office."

"It must have come loose. I was so distracted— Who do you suppose found it and knew it was mine?"

Gregg looked at her, decided she could take it. "My first thought is whoever did this."

"You mean—" She swallowed. "You mean they were watching me?"

"So it would appear."

She swayed and he reached out to catch her arm. She drew away from him, pushed aside the barricade tape. "I'm all right," she said. "Let's get this over with."

Gregg stayed at his office until late into the night. The report Karen had filed with Jack a couple of months earlier lay scattered across his desk along with a folder from the *Clarion* that contained recent articles she'd written. The more he read, the more bitter his self-recrimination became.

He walked over to a window. *How could he face her after all the groundless accusations and charges he'd thrown at her?* And more than that. *How could he tell her how much he'd come to care for her?* She'd laugh in his face, as any sane woman would.

Dear God, I need your help again. There has to be some way to make things right with Karen. I need her too much to let her go.

Karen pulled into the driveway and saw with disappointment that Gregg's truck was still gone. She got out and began unloading boxes and bags and carrying them into the duplex. When she finished she locked the car and went into her room to lay down across the bed in the sheltering darkness.

It seemed only moments later that the door burst open and the overhead light flashed on. Gregg stood in the doorway staring at her, his face white. Karen sat up in confusion. "Gregg?"

He crossed the room and pulled her into his arms. "Thank God, you're all right!" He held her closer. "When I saw your tires slashed I went crazy. I'm so sorry. I know your work is important and I know someone is trying to hurt you. I should never have left you alone."

She pulled away from him. Wet her lips. "My tires are slashed?" She glanced at the clock, her eyes wide with fear. "It had to have happened in the last half hour. I didn't hear anything. I guess I fell asleep." She walked over to the window, glanced out, then back at Gregg. "Whoever it is, I'm not safe anywhere, am I?" Her broken whisper cut Gregg like a knife. "Not even here, in your protective custody!"

The plane rolled down the grass runway, picked up speed, then lifted off. After a short climb, it turned left to fly over the lake, rocked its wings in farewell and turned to a south-southeast heading.

Gregg leaned back comfortably and reached into the back for his thermos of coffee.

"I can do that," Karen offered. She poured coffee into the cup and replaced the cap. Gregg took it and sipped appreciatively.

"I never realize how much I miss Marie's coffee until I have to drink my own for awhile," he commented.

Unconsciously, Karen wrinkled her nose in distaste. Gregg caught the gesture and grinned.

"So why is it you don't like coffee?" he asked, putting his cup in a holder and reaching for a sectional.

"I guess my mother stressed it too much. Drinking coffee seemed to be socially acceptable. I usually chose the least preferred thing to do." She shrugged. "Even in choosing my career, I suppose."

Gregg cleared his throat. "About that—"

Karen cringed. *Here it comes*, she thought. *Some new barb concerning reporters.*

Again Gregg saw her reaction and a puzzled frown creased his brow. *What did she think he might say?*

"Last night I tried to catch up on the last six months of your articles," he said. "You never told me you were a one woman crusade."

She closed her eyes. "Please, Gregg. Today is going to be difficult enough without your making fun of me—"

"I'm not making fun of you!" He stared at her.

"Of course you are—"

"Karen! The work you've been doing is great. The youth center, the nursing home, the children's home, the day care—I had no idea you were a consumer advocate."

"I'm not a consumer advocate," she said through clenched teeth. "I do get a lot of leads from mail addressed to my column, but all I do is write stories."

"So which of these fascinating stories do you think has gotten you in trouble? Or, rather, earned you the wrath of someone—"

"The calls and threats started during the series on the nursing home. But it isn't logical that anyone could object to that, is it? I mean—"

"Someone has vandalized your home, your office, your car, would have done who knows what if you'd been there." Gregg shook his head. "I don't think you're going to find logic driving this person's actions."

Karen didn't reply, and Gregg sighed wearily. "I read the series on the nursing home last night. I didn't realize how much I owe you."

She looked at him. "You owe me?" she repeated.

"Yes. My grandmother is there. She broke her hip and needed specialized care. We thought she would get it, but she fell a couple of times.

We were about to find someplace else when it suddenly got better. Now I know why."

"Angela is your grandmother," Karen said. "I knew her name was McClaren, but at the time I didn't connect it with you." She swallowed. "She said she's going home soon."

"Yes. As a matter-of-fact, Mom's coming to get her this weekend and stay at the duplex with her. If all goes well, she'll take her back to the ranch. If not, she'll stay there for a few more weeks."

"It sounds as if I should make plans to vacate by the weekend," Karen said. Why did that thought hurt, somehow?

"Not necessary," Gregg said. "You're coming to Telluride with me and the twins."

She drew in her breath. "We've been over that, already! I have no intention of going anywhere—"

"You're still in protective custody," Gregg said. "I'll make it official, if necessary."

"Is that why it hasn't worked very well?" Karen asked. "Because it hasn't been official?"

"It hasn't worked very well because one of the parties hasn't taken it seriously," Gregg replied. "Did I want you to go off alone last night?"

"I had things to do. So did you. We couldn't have done them all if we stayed together."

"That explanation wouldn't have done me any good if anything had happened to you." Gregg let out his breath. "You must have been followed from your apartment. We've pretty much established that it's being watched."

"Do you think the duplex is, too?"

"I know it is. By our guys. I called them last night."

"Did you have my car towed away?"

"Yes. It will be repaired and stored until we return next week."

"Will your mother and grandmother be safe in the duplex?" Karen asked, watching his face.

His jaw tightened. "If I have any doubt, they won't be staying there."

"All this would be so much simpler if I just went back to Kansas," Karen sighed.

She felt his glance. "Give me a chance. If you still want to go after this weekend, I won't try to stop you."

Karen felt her throat tighten and swallowed around a sudden lump.

They flew in silence for some time, each absorbed in their own thoughts. Finally, Gregg sighed and glanced at his watch. "We still have a couple of hours to kill. Tell me about some of the other patients in the nursing home."

Karen thought for a moment. "Well, I mentioned Rosa in one of the articles. She's a lovely Jewish lady—"

"The diabetic. They had trouble regulating her medication because she refused to eat anything that wasn't kosher."

Karen nodded.

"Why was she in this nursing home, in particular?"

"What do you mean?"

"Well, in this instance, I can almost sympathize with the staff. I know they have to be able to handle special diets for medical reasons, but there are many Jewish supported nursing homes where she would have probably been more comfortable, and there wouldn't have been a problem with the diet. Is it a question of money?"

"I don't think so. From what I gather she's quiet wealthy. And she only has one living relative, a rather unpleasant nephew. He visited a couple of times while I was there."

"Doesn't that sound like a motive to you?" Gregg asked.

"Doesn't what sound like a motive?" Karen turned to look at him, found him watching her intently.

He grinned. "Hey, you're the reporter here. Don't make me do all the work." Then he sobered. "He might not have found it in his best interest that she be well taken care of. You might have thrown a monkey wrench into his carefully contrived plans."

Karen closed her eyes. "Slow down. Let me see if I can catch up. He knows she's diabetic. He knows she adheres strictly to a kosher diet. He puts her somewhere where, even with the best of intentions, a nursing home would have trouble dealing with her." Karen smiled. "And she is a bit arrogant. She's not anyone's favorite patient."

Gregg looked at her. "It sounds as if you admire her."

"Maybe I do. I've never been anyone's favorite anything. Anyway, there's no one else in the family to check on her, to make sure she's being properly cared for, and he doesn't care. Theoretically, of course."

"Except you came along."

"Actually, I got a request, a case history, as it were. Someone wanted me to check out the conditions there." Karen shivered. "Angela was in a bad way when I arrived."

Gregg tensed. "What do you mean?"

"She had just fallen again the first time I showed up. They treated it like getting back on a horse after you've been thrown. They put a lot of pressure on her and I could see she was very nervous about it."

"What happened then?" he asked.

Karen shifted uncomfortably. This wasn't the time for the truth. She pretended to misunderstand the question.

"Well, after a while, I got the healthier patients organized into a support group for the less fortunate. Someone always walked with Angela. That's all she needed, just the assurance that she wasn't alone. They saw that Rosa ate properly."

"Before this support group came into play," Gregg prompted. "Who watched out for Angela? Who encouraged her?"

"I would hope you did," Karen replied evasively.

"I had blinders on an inch thick," Gregg said in disgust. "If it had been up to me, she would probably still be lying in bed. No, I remember her talking about a lovely girl who came in to walk with her every day. A girl who told her she couldn't live the rest of her life looking over her shoulder; who—instead of fearing falling—made her look at it as a challenge not to fall. You wouldn't know anything about that, would you?"

"Why would I?" Karen asked, her voice strained.

"Because, my love, that girl was you. It couldn't have been anyone else." He shook his head. "Boy, did I ever have blinders on!" he muttered under his breath.

Karen held her breath for a moment. When Gregg spoke again, he did not pursue the subject.

"What about Rosa's nephew?" he asked. "Shall I have Jack check him out?"

Karen shook her head. "I'd hate to destroy someone's life on a hunch—even if it does seem to have some merit."

Father Brian McFeld and his sister, Katrina, met them at the airport in Lamar. Karen slipped into a near trance, feeling as if everything happening was out of her control. She recognized her state as a protective reaction, shielding her against the pain she knew would come.

It seemed only moments before they arrived at a lovely suburban home. The McFelds introduced them to Juliana's parents, and her brother, Matt. They met Julie, too, there to offer comfort to her best friend's family. Karen felt she knew them all intimately. She could not shake a sense of guilt that she at least was there under false pretenses.

Listening unobtrusively to the exchanges, Karen learned that Juliana's boyfriend was named Bobby. He and Matt were classmates, juniors in high school. After what seemed ages, but must have been only moments, another car pulled into the drive and a young man helped a sobbing woman into the house. They were introduced as Bobby's mother and brother and Juliana's family immediately enfolded them in loving embraces.

Karen gravitated to a window on the other side of the room. Katrina McFeld joined her there and touched her hand gently. Karen smiled gratefully and Katrina nodded her understanding. They both were outsiders. Father McFeld and Gregg had a duty to perform as part of their jobs. They belonged here. She and Katrina were only here because of the men they loved.

Katrina led her into the kitchen where she began finding equipment and ingredients for making coffee.

"There is a sadness about you, my dear," Katrina said as she measured coffee.

Karen shrugged. "It's a sad day."

"It is that. But your sadness seems more personal. Something to do with Officer Watson perhaps?"

Karen sucked in her breath. "What do you mean?"

"Are you in love with him?"

Karen started to laugh and broke off, realizing the inappropriateness of such a sound. She shook her head. "Love Gregg Watson? As if there might be a future in that."

"Our hearts aren't usually as logical as our minds," Katrina said. "I've seen you watching him. You hurt for him, and you wouldn't feel that way unless you cared a great deal."

"Oh, I care all right."

"And how does he feel?"

Karen shook her head again. "I have no way to judge anything he says or does except in the most negative of contexts. I have no idea how he feels."

"Have you prayed about this?"

Karen looked at her. "Prayed about what?"

"Have you asked God to guide you in this relationship, to help you understand what drives Gregg. He obviously has a lot of sadness in his life, too."

Karen nodded. "Yes. He has lost several people very close to him. I think he has trouble trusting anyone to be around for the long haul."

"And you? Would you be willing to be there for the long haul?"

Karen swallowed. Forced a slight smile. "He only has to ask."

An hour later, Gregg found Karen and Katrina in the kitchen talking quietly as they put cups on a tray.

"Good idea," he approved. "I'm sure everyone will appreciate some coffee about now."

"I know Brian needs some," Katrina said in her quiet voice. "Can you carry this tray, Gregg? I'll get the smaller one. Karen, dear, hold the door for Gregg."

As she moved to obey, Karen realized that Katrina must be very familiar with this routine. Quiet, efficient, and organized, she began to restore order and impart the sense that life would go on. *And all by the simple act of making coffee.*

Katrina drove them back to the airport a couple of hours later, leaving her brother with the bereaved families for a bit longer. She hugged both Gregg and Karen. Gregg thanked her for her help throughout the ordeal. She merely nodded and wished them a safe trip home.

CHAPTER TEN

And now they were back at the ranch. Karen looked out over the lake at the setting sun as the plane swooped in for a landing. Gregg hadn't said a dozen words during the entire return flight. She understood his need to be alone with his thoughts, and she did not intrude. However, she desperately needed someone to talk to, someone who would understand her own turbulent feelings. And Gregg was the only one who could understand.

It did not surprise her that he headed for the lake as soon as he finished taking care of the plane. Feeling lost and forlorn, Karen picked up her bag and made her way to the house.

Anna looked up from the sink as Karen pushed open the door. Not expecting to see anyone, Karen had no time to try and compose herself. She read the concern and alarm on Anna's face.

"My dear—" Anna came to her, caught her hands. "Where's Gregg?"

"I think he took the boat out," Karen managed to say, her voice tight.

"That bad, huh?" Anna said with a sad smile.

Karen looked at her. "Did he tell you—"

"I only know you went to visit the families of the teenagers who were killed a couple of weeks ago. That you helped Gregg with the identification." Anna led her into the den. "Sit here and I'll get a fire going. It's gotten cold since the sun set. Would you like some hot cocoa?"

Karen felt herself slipping into a state of numbness as Anna bustled around her. The cocoa tasted wonderful and she began to grow warm. *And drowsy. So wonderfully sleepy.* The fire had a tranquilizing effect, peaceful and lulling. She thought she heard voices but found it too difficult to concentrate.

"I gave her a mild sedative," Anna said to Gregg, reaching up to touch his haggard face. "She looked on the verge of collapse." She searched his eyes anxiously. "And how are you holding up?"

He shook his head. "This job doesn't get any easier," he said. "Why do I keep doing it?"

"You don't have to, you know," Anna said. "There's nothing I want more than for you to come back here and settle down, where you belong."

"You know I want that, too," Gregg said. "But not by myself. I can't stay here alone. And I haven't found anyone willing to share my Eden." He frowned for a moment, trying to recall who had called it that. "Anyway—"

"You've found her, Gregg. You know that as well as I do," Anna's eyes were bright as she looked up at him. "Just make sure she knows before it's too late."

Gregg stood looking down at Karen as she lay curled in a corner of the sofa. One arm crooked beneath her head, the other hand clutched a blanket pulled beneath her chin. Her hair tumbled over the pillows. The firelight playing on her face made her eyelashes look dark and feathery as they lay against her cheeks.

He sat down beside her and reached out to push the hair back from her face. He trailed his knuckles down her cheek and brushed his thumb across her lips. His hand trembled slightly and he drew it back, afraid that in the next moment he might pull her into his arms. He wanted to kiss her with all the longing that had been building for days now, perhaps weeks. At least, ever since he'd seen her again in the park.

He turned away and drew a hand slowly down his face. Her mission was over. She had helped him identify Juliana and Bobby. He no longer had any reason to keep her near him, except the protective custody charade, and that would be over as soon as they found the culprit. She'd talked about going back to Kansas. How could he keep her here? How could he convince her that this could be her Eden, too, if she would only claim it?

He looked at her again, and then with a groan, he reached for her and pulled her onto his lap, cradling her against his chest. This might be all he would have, but at least he'd have this moment to remember. The feel of her warmth and softness as he held her next to his heart.

Dear God, don't let me hurt Karen any more. Help me show her how much I care. And give me the courage to make room in my life for her.

Karen awakened feeling groggy and listless. She had slept in the same room at the ranch she'd used before, although she didn't remember coming upstairs. She threw back the covers to find herself wearing a strange T-shirt. Her clothes lay neatly over the back of a chair.

She made her way to the shower, her head beginning to ache slightly. She let the water run over her body for what seemed ages, until she realized it wasn't making her feel better. Still feeling detached, she dried off and got dressed.

"There you are, my dear!" Anna greeted quietly when Karen entered the kitchen. "I was beginning to get a little worried."

"Why would you be worried? What time is it? I guess I overslept—"

"That isn't your fault," Anna said, shaking her head. "You seemed so upset last night, I gave you a mild sedative in your cocoa. It never occurred to me that it would knock you out so soundly. I just wanted you to relax a little."

Karen stared at her, pushed her hair back restlessly. "So that's it. I should have recognized the symptoms." She shrugged. "No real harm done. It'll just take a few hours to shake off the after effects."

"Karen, I'm sorry—" Anna began.

"Don't worry about it." Karen began pacing. "Do you know when Gregg plans to leave?"

"Not for a couple of hours. He's down at the barn now. Then he's coming back to have breakfast. Why don't you walk down and join him? Fresh air might make you feel better."

"It might," Karen agreed. *But being around Gregg wouldn't.* She didn't tell Anna that. "Would it be all right if I had some juice, or something? I don't remember having dinner. By the way, how did I get to bed?"

"Gregg carried you upstairs and I undressed you. I borrowed one of Kelly's T-shirts for you to sleep in, rather than go through your bag."

Karen took the juice Anna held out to her, met her eyes briefly. "Thanks for telling me." She sipped the juice. "I think I will go for a walk, maybe down to the lake."

"You do that. I'm making breakfast. It'll be ready when you get back."

"Where's Marie?" Karen turned back to ask.

"I gave her the rest of the week off. I'm driving back with you and Gregg. He told you that we're bringing Mother back to the duplex for the weekend?"

Karen nodded. "Did he tell you that I know your mother? I met her at the nursing home."

"That's wonderful!" Anna said. "I had no idea. I wonder if you could be the girl she's talked about so much—"

Karen turned away, sorry she had mentioned it. "I won't be long."

Anna looked after her, a frown of concern creasing her brow. Something was bothering Karen. Something a lot bigger than what she had gone through yesterday. Something, Anna feared, that had to do with Gregg.

The boat was gone, Karen noted immediately. Well, in that case, it would probably be safe to go to the barn. Last week Kelly had mentioned that a mare was due to foal any day and the kittens she'd seen then didn't have their eyes open yet. Maybe they would by now.

The foal had arrived. It stood on long, wobbly legs, a few days old. After gazing at it for several minutes, Karen went in search of the kittens. They were harder to find now that they could find their way in the big world. She located them in an empty stall and sat down with her back against a bale of hay, letting them climb over her as they would. A smile touched her lips.

"I've heard of someone going to the dogs," Gregg said, his voice coming from above her. "Is this known as going to the cats?"

Karen jumped, startling the kittens, who went scurrying to the safety of their mother. Karen stood and brushed off her slacks, looking anywhere but at Gregg.

"I saw the new foal," she said. "How old is it?"

"He's three days old. Born last Sunday right after we left. Both mother and son are doing great."

"I'm glad." She swallowed. She couldn't go on not looking at him, and she couldn't keep making small talk. At last, reluctantly, she raised her eyes to his, to find him watching her, waiting, his arms folded on the door to the stall.

As if sensing her reluctance to be alone with him, Gregg opened the door. "Are you ready to go back?"

As she neared the door he stepped back, making sure she had room to pass without touching him. He closed the door.

Karen walked out into the freshness of early morning. Her head had cleared, but she found herself wishing for something to numb her senses. Being around Gregg took a toll on her emotions that she could ill afford. She didn't know how she would make it through the drive back to town.

"When are we going back?" she asked.

"After we have breakfast and as soon as Mom is ready. She's going—"

"She told me." Maybe having Anna along would help. *Maybe not.* She turned toward the house.

"Karen," Gregg's voice was reluctant. "Do you have a moment?"

She turned back, her brows raised. "You know that better than I do. I'm afraid I'm at your mercy here."

"I'm sorry about yesterday."

She shrugged. "What is there to apologize for? It had to be done and I insisted on going—"

"That isn't what I meant."

She looked down. "I'm not sure—"

"I'm talking about the way I shut you out on the trip back. I know you needed to talk. I just couldn't stop replaying the times they came to tell us about Megan and my dad. And the time we all waited to hear about Rock. It's just that I know so well how those people felt yesterday—"

"And you don't think I did?" Karen asked.

He drew in his breath. "I didn't say that—"

"But obviously you thought it. If you weren't willing to share those feelings with me, it must have been because you didn't think I could understand them." She drew a deep steadying breath. "I wish I could be the cold, calculating, unfeeling wretch you think I am. I would like so much to not care for you—maybe even to dislike you."

Karen shook her head. "Unfortunately for me, I'm naive, trusting, and inexperienced. And in spite of everything cruel and hurtful you've said to me, I've still managed to fall in love with you." She laughed, a harsh bitter sound. "I guess I should have put stupid at the top of my list."

She raised her head and straightened her shoulders. "But as they say, we live and learn. I can try to become that person you insist on believing me to be. It gives me something to strive for." She shook her head. "Maybe even my mother would be proud of me."

"Karen!" Gregg caught her arm and pulled her around to face him.

"Let go of me!"

"Not until you listen—"

"I don't want you to talk to me! You only say things that hurt—"

His eyes darkened. "Okay. I won't talk." He pulled her toward him.

"No, Gregg, please!" She whispered.

He held her face between his hands, staring into her eyes. "You can't have it both ways," he said huskily, brushing his thumb across her lips. "If you won't let me tell you how I feel, then you'll have to let me show you."

"No—" she said again, but as her lips parted, his mouth came down and closed over them, hard and then softening, giving as well as taking. His arms went around her, drawing her closer.

Karen felt herself falling and reached out for his shoulders, clinging to him. Her arms crept around his neck, and her mouth moved to answer his. Time and space became one and Gregg was all that existed for her.

CHAPTER ELEVEN

Karen listened to the talk between Gregg and Anna as the truck sped through the brilliant afternoon. They were only a few miles from town. Gregg planned to drop Anna off at the nursing home as they passed it and then he would return for her and his grandmother in the station wagon.

Karen tried to plan her next move, but since Gregg's kiss this morning, she hadn't been able to think at all. Perhaps that had been his intention. When at last he put her away from him, reaching out to steady her as she swayed, his words had been cryptic.

"Don't talk," he said. *"Don't think. Just feel. Feel my arms around you, my lips on yours. Decide whether or not you like that feeling, because we are going to talk about this again. Not today—probably not tomorrow. But before the weekend is over. And you are going to Telluride. Don't even think about saying no. And just so you understand, I want you to come—more than I've wanted anything in a long time. I've wanted you to come*

all along. I was just afraid to tell you how much."

As the truck neared the nursing home, a police car with siren and flashing lights raced around them. Gregg tensed, and reached for his phone. He punched in a number.

"Jack, this is Gregg. I just got back in town and a cruiser raced passed. What's up?"

"A 9-1-1 from the nursing home. Your hunch paid off. Everyone is fine and Mr. Marcus has been subdued. We're on our way to pick him up."

"I'll be there in about three minutes," Gregg said.

Karen had heard Jack's voice clearly. She spoke now for the first time in hours. "What hunch?" she asked, her voice strained.

He glanced at her. "Sorry I didn't tell you. Last night I called Jack and told him about Rosa and her nephew. He did a background check and found that he's up to his neck in gambling debts. I asked him to post someone at the nursing home for awhile. I never thought anything would happen this fast."

"It's because I wasn't there," Karen said.

"What do you mean?"

"I stop by a couple of nights a week. For the last month I haven't been able to. He thinks he scared me off. It was safe to move on her."

"Then you aren't upset—"

"You get paid to play hunches," Karen said. "I don't."

Gregg had to be satisfied with that, but Anna saw his knuckles whiten on the steering wheel. She put a hand on his arm in silent understanding.

As they reached the nursing home, the door burst open and two uniformed officers dragged a screaming, raging man down the steps. Small and unkempt, his curly hair stood out in all directions. He stopped abruptly, almost pulling one of the officers off balance. Handcuffs hampered his gesture as he stared straight at Karen.

"It's her fault!" he shrieked. "It's all her fault. If she'd just minded her own business!" The words kept echoing across the parking lot as the officers moved him out of range.

Gregg moved instinctively to shield Karen while the officers hauled the man away. She turned her face into his shoulder and he felt her draw a shuddering breath.

"Okay?" he whispered.

She raised her head. Nodded. "Let's see how everyone is. This must have been upsetting—"

But as they moved through the door, no sobbing hysterics greeted them as Karen had feared. On the contrary, both nurses and patients seemed to be congratulating one another, quite pleased with themselves.

As she stared around, bemused, someone spotted Karen and called her name. "There's Karen! So glad you're back—"

"And my daughter and grandson with her!" Angela's rich voice sounded above the others. "Come here, my dear! Let's have a look at you."

And before she could protest, Karen found herself pulled into the circle. Angela relinquished her and turned back to Gregg and Anna. Her eyes bright and twinkling, her step firm, she crossed to greet them both with a hug.

"You've missed all the excitement," she said. "But where did you find Karen? I haven't seen her for weeks."

124

Gregg grinned at her. "Well, actually she's been helping me with a case, and I've been helping her with one."

Angela studied him for a moment. "Sounds like a match made in heaven," she pronounced.

Anna laughed. "Doesn't it? But right now I wouldn't ask Karen where she thinks it originated." Then, "How are you, Mother? Are you ready to try civilian life again?"

"Ready, willing, and able. Just try to stop me." Her face clouded for a moment. "I hope they'll be okay here without me." Then her face brightened. "They will be. Karen's back."

Anna took her arm. "Let's go get you packed."

Karen sat beside the bed, holding the thin hand in hers. The frail woman in the bed had been heavily sedated. But before she closed her eyes, she had recognized Karen and smiled weakly at her. Now Karen sat beside her, unwilling to think what might have happened if Gregg had not followed his gut instincts. It would have been her fault—

She felt a movement and looked up to see Gregg in the doorway, his shoulders filling the space. He came toward her and knelt to catch her hand.

"They say she'll be fine," he whispered.

Karen nodded. She placed Rosa's hand back on the bed and released it, allowing Gregg to draw her to her feet.

"He—he tried to smother her with a pillow," she whispered. "Thanks to you, he didn't succeed."

He shook his head. "Thanks to you," he said. He put his arm around her shoulders to lead her to the door.

Just inside and still out of sight, Karen turned to him. She caught the front of his jacket and looked into his eyes. "My hero!" she said, her lashes lowering demurely.

She felt his arms tighten briefly, then his hands on her arms. "Rosa is very special to you, isn't she?"

"She is. I adopt a lot of people. She's the grandmother I never had."

"I'd like to offer you Angela as the grandmother you can still have," Gregg said, trailing his finger lightly down her nose.

Karen stared at him. "We weren't going to talk about this just yet," she reminded, her voice a husky whisper.

"Okay, we won't." He grinned. *"Just yet."* He released her and followed her out of the room.

A nurse wheeled Angela down the ramp and Karen stopped in shock. Apparently Gregg had already gone to the duplex and exchanged his truck for the shiny station wagon waiting at the door. He installed Angela in the back seat with Anna, tossed her luggage in, and climbed behind the wheel.

He looked at Karen. "It's safe to pick up your car now."

She twisted her fingers together. "I'm in no hurry." She raised her head. "Except I do have one errand to run tomorrow—before we leave."

"I know. Delivering the Easter Baskets." Gregg glanced in the rear view mirror at his grandmother. "I saw them, in all their glory." A short pause. "I'll go with you." He turned the key.

"No, really—" Karen started to protest, to be drowned out by the engine starting. She relaxed back into her seat, a smile playing around her mouth.

"Let him go," Angela said, watching Karen. "It'll be good for him. He's been entirely too sheltered and spoiled."

Karen didn't know that she agreed, but she knew she wanted him to go with her to deliver the Easter Baskets to the children's home.

Gregg went into the office the next morning and Karen remembered another errand she had to run. She borrowed the station wagon and returned just as Gregg pulled into the drive. He came over to open the door for her.

"Don't tell me you went without me?" he said.

"Of course not. I needed to get a couple of things for the trip that I still had in storage." She went around to unlock the back of the car.

"Uh." Gregg looked at the assortment of bags and bundles. "You do know we have limited storage space with four people on the plane?"

"I know that. I wasn't sure which bag I needed."

He nodded. "We'll leave after we play Easter Bunny, spend the night with Kelly and Kyle and leave at daybreak for Telluride."

Karen nodded. "It sounds as if you've done this before."

"Actually, no. But it sounds like a plan." He grabbed a bag in each hand and started up the drive, leaving Karen staring after him.

They managed to sneak the Easter Baskets in unobserved and Karen spent the next hour introducing Gregg to the children she had grown close to in the past year and a half. To her surprise, he already knew several of the older boys through sports activities that were sponsored by the police department. One young man in particular seemed to idolize Gregg, and Karen could see that Gregg returned his affection.

Karen's own particular favorite was a seven year old girl with auburn curls and green eyes. At the moment she had both front teeth missing, and Karen found her totally adorable. She showed Karen the gift the tooth fairy left, a bracelet Karen recognized as once having been her own. She had left instructions that it be given to Amanda when her teeth came out.

Karen looked up and found Gregg watching her as she admired Amanda's bracelet. She held his gaze before turning back to the little girl.

"So tell me," Gregg said, "was Amanda's bracelet another gift from your mother?"

Karen straightened. They had been on the road a half hour and had maintained a comfortable silence. She wasn't going to let Gregg ruin things.

"Of course not," she replied. "If I gave her something I didn't care for anyway, it would have no meaning."

"Did your mother ever give you anything you cared for?"

"I don't want to talk about my mother," she said.

"Okay. What would you like to talk about?"

"Michael."

"Michael?" He glanced at her.

"He idolizes you."

"He's a great kid." A shrug. "There are people who like me, you know. My mom—"

"What I saw was a lot more than like. How did you meet him?" Karen turned so that she could see his face.

"I work with Big Brothers off and on. I've taken him to a couple of ball games. And I took him flying once."

"Why him in particular?"

Gregg's answer took awhile. "I knew his parents," he said. "His dad was a cop. They were killed in a car wreck returning from a vacation trip. I guess I feel responsible. They had no other family." He paused. "So what's Amanda's story?"

"Her mother put her up for adoption at birth. She's been in and out of foster homes. I tried to adopt her about six months ago."

"You what?" Gregg's voice was incredulous.

"Get real, Gregg," Karen said. "It's being done all the time. A lot of career women with good incomes who have given up having children of their own are beginning to adopt. You'll be happy to know they turned me down. Apparently a reporter is either too unstable, or not respectable enough."

"Says who?"

"How do I know who?" Her voice was impatient. "The adoption board—or whatever it's called."

"I'm surprised you don't know the names and addresses of everyone on the board. You haven't given up on anything else." His voice was crisp, factual.

"I haven't given up on this. I just got sidetracked by my mother's illness. As a matter-of-fact—" she hesitated.

"You're thinking that with your inheritance you might be considered stable enough. Anyone who could offer a little girl a fortune—"

"Maybe I should stop thinking of my inheritance as something evil, something guaranteed to make me unhappy. I could do good things with it. Both my sisters have children. I could see that they get good educations. And *maybe* I could adopt Amanda." She lapsed into silence.

"Karen." Gregg hesitated, fearing he treaded on sacred ground. "Why are you so sure your mother wanted you to be unhappy? I know you said you don't want to talk about her—"

"She never wanted me, and she never missed an opportunity to point out how much she didn't want me—not me in particular. Just children in general."

"Yet she had other children after you?"

"She allowed herself to be used by the men she became involved with. My father was also to blame for insisting she provide him with an heir."

"How do you explain your sisters?"

"I can't."

"Is it possible she might have loved your step-father?"

"No."

"Then why marry him if she already had money and everything she could possibly want?"

"He made an attractive escort to all the social functions she attended."

Gregg let out his breath in a sharp whistle. "You are one cynical lady!"

"Yeah, well, tell me how I can be anything else."

She saw Gregg's hands tighten on the steering wheel and a muscle clench in his jaw. "Karen, for the most part, you saw your mother for what she was. Don't let her opinion define you. You know your own worth."

"Yeah, right," she said dryly.

"Okay," he grated. "I haven't been that good for your self image. I'm more than willing to admit I've been wrong. On second thought, why listen to me in the first place?"

"Because your opinion matters," Karen said. "I know it makes no sense, but it always has." She shrugged, tried to speak lightly. "Well, at least you kept me on my toes. Actually, I'd begun to enjoy our little encounters."

"I didn't. You threatened all the big, tough, macho nonsense I believed about myself."

"That's impossible!" Karen said with total conviction.

"But true, non-the-less." He grinned. "You always got in the last word, you know, and left me fuming incoherently."

"Words are the only weapons I have."

"Well, they can be deadly in your hands."

She studied him from beneath her lashes. "Gregg, if I tell you how much I admire and respect you, with absolute sincerity, do you think you can let me know you; let me into that world where you hide the real Gregg Watson. I promise to leave my weapons behind."

He reached for her hand, squeezed it gently and released it. "I think we can negotiate something to our mutual satisfaction."

Karen sat on the dock, a gentle breeze playing with her hair. Gregg was having one last talk with the foreman before leaving. A smile touched her lips. Whatever rules he now played by, Gregg had been the epitome of attentiveness and courtesy since their arrival at the ranch.

She'd never had any doubt that Gregg could turn on the charm at will. She'd seen it often enough, but always for the benefit of someone else. This was the first time she'd been privileged to be the recipient herself, and the effect left her slightly detached, as if she weren't really a part of it all, but would wake up to find the old Gregg firmly entrenched.

With a sigh she stood up and turned back for one last look at the lake.

"Have you figured it out?" Gregg asked behind her.

She looked at him. "Figured what out?"

He studied her, his eyes serious. Finally he shrugged. "Nothing, I guess. I thought perhaps you felt it, too."

"Felt what?"

"The magic of the lake. The enchantment. Whatever it is that gets in your blood and won't let go."

"I do find it soothing—I guess that's the right word." She glanced back at the water. "I wondered what it is that seems to hold *you* in its spell."

He grinned. "At least you're curious. There may still be hope. Are you ready to get started?"

She looked up, opened her mouth to speak, closed it, her eyes troubled.

"Now what?" Gregg crossed the dock to put his hands on her arms.

"It's not too late to change your mind about taking me along," she said. "I don't want to spoil this weekend. I'm not sure—"

"How could you possibly spoil it?" Gregg asked. "Except by not coming." He gave her a gentle shake. His eyes were warm, caressing. "I promise to be on my best behavior. What more can you ask?"

Staring into his laughing gaze, Karen felt her throat constrict. She swallowed and unconsciously moistened her lips. She saw his eyes darken and he reached to tip her face up.

"Perhaps I made that promise too soon," he murmured. "All I can think about is how much I want to kiss you—" His arms slipped around her. "I haven't thought of much else since yesterday morning."

"Neither have I," Karen whispered.

"Do you think we should do something about it?" His eyes smiled down at her, teasing, caring.

She traced a fingertip across his lips as she had done so often in her dreams. She loved his mouth. She loved him. Her fingers trembled.

"I don't know," she said, lowering her hand, to rest it against his chest.

His hand came up to close over hers. He brought it to his mouth, brushed his lips across her palm and felt her tremble.

"Darling?" The word was a prayer, a statement, a question. He bent his head and his lips caressed hers tentatively. Seeking. Finding.

"Yes—" The word broke on a sob as her arms wound around his neck, pulling him closer. The caress became a possession as his mouth seemed to draw the life from her, only to return it again filled with sweetness and a promise such as she had never known.

CHAPTER TWELVE

Gregg glanced over at Karen in the seat beside him. They had been flying for a couple of hours and the drone of the engine had lulled her to sleep. He felt he should pinch himself to make sure he was awake, and that she was really here with him.

Dear God, don't let me blow this, he murmured a little repetitive prayer. Now that he had finally gotten her away from a world that put too much pressure on them both, he had to convince her that he couldn't live without her—or perhaps that she couldn't go on without him.

He remembered her words from the day before. *". . . in spite of everything cruel and hurtful you've said to me, I've still managed to fall in love with you."* Had she meant the words she had spoken and were they still true? They had to be. He couldn't love her in this all consuming way without her returning those feelings.

Karen studied Gregg through her lashes. He constantly scanned the surrounding airspace and checked the folded sectional clipped in front of him. Dark aviator glasses obscured his eyes. His leather jacket lent an air of mystery and sex appeal that played havoc with her senses. She wanted him so much that it hurt. At the same time, she knew the improbability of them permanently putting aside their differences.

Of course that kiss a little while ago had worked wonders toward patching up their relationship. That she loved Gregg, Karen had no doubt. She gave a mental shrug. She had also loved her step-father and she had still lost him. She had even loved her mother, difficult though that proved to be.

"How much for your thoughts?" Gregg asked, suddenly looking at her.

She jumped. "How did you know I was awake?"

"You're too restless. The only time you relax is when you're asleep."

"That's probably true."

"Trust me—" he broke off. "On the other hand, maybe it takes my mother drugging you to get you to relax."

"That's right. She told me you carried me up to bed the other night."

"Does that bother you?"

"A little. It's a very vulnerable feeling to know that someone has been watching you while you sleep."

"I guess it is." Gregg fell silent.

"How much longer?" Karen asked after a moment.

He glanced at his watch. "Thirty minutes—probably closer to twenty. Are you getting hungry?"

"I don't know. Should I be?"

He sighed. "How would I know? I haven't seen you eat enough to keep a bird alive since you went home and found your apartment vandalized. Grandmother said you've lost weight."

"She worries too much."

"Only about people she cares for. And you seem to be pretty high on that list."

"I am a little hungry," Karen said. "Why?"

"Kelly said they were taking us to some fancy restaurant—"

"Fancy?" Karen's eyes widened in horror.

Gregg grinned. "Fancy to a nineteen-year-old means you have to wear shoes to get in. I gather your definition of a fancy restaurant is rather different than theirs. Or mine."

"Rather," Karen agreed. "Actually, I wouldn't care if I never see another fancy restaurant, by my definition, that is. I grew up in a society where your value hinged on the clothes you wore, the car you drove, the places you ate. When you said earlier that I know my own worth, I don't, not really. Not worth as Angela, or Anna, or even you would define it. I've been trying to discover it."

"It can't be that hard. What are you worth to your family, your fellow man, to society?"

"Since I left my mother, my worth has been tied up in my job. It shouldn't come as a surprise to you that your opinion of reporters is a majority opinion."

Gregg sighed, long and eloquently.

"Unfortunately, it's even deserved—but only in a minority of cases."

"Karen—" Gregg began, then broke off as if unsure how to continue. "I don't suppose you would believe—" He stopped again. Another sigh. "I was attracted to you from the first. Every instinct told me you were all wrong for me. I had such a lousy track record with women, even those I felt could fit into my life, that I didn't see anything working out with you. Everything I ever said to you was defensive, to counter the attraction. I'm sure that doesn't make any sense to you. I'm sorry."

She looked at him, eyes narrowed. "Did it help?"

"Not so as I could tell," he said. "I used to cruise by all the hot spots when a story broke on the off chance I might run into you."

Karen laughed softly.

"What's so funny?"

"Just that I used to ask for all the juicy assignments on the possibility you might be there. I tried to think up situations I could get into so that you'd be forced to rescue me, like you did that first time."

"When you were covering the riot and that gang of thugs had you cornered. That's as close to Hell as I ever hope to be. You seemed to get quite a kick out of it." A scowl furrowed his brow.

"Did you think I'd let you, or them, know how frightened I was? If I never properly thanked you, then I will now. I am very grateful that you rescued me, even if my life hasn't been quite the same since."

He glanced at her and she could tell that he was frowning behind his dark glasses. "You can thank me *properly* later. I'm afraid it's gonna take more than words after all these years."

"Hey, be grateful for what you get. You don't know how much the words cost." But her eyes were smiling, her voice light, as she looked at him.

Gregg leaned across the space separating them and kissed her softly.

Karen stiffened. "What was that for?" Her voice was husky, uncertain.

Gregg straightened, returned to his flying. "Payment on account," he said tersely.

Karen could not have replied if her life depended on it. She made a restless movement and turned back to the window.

Kelly and Kyle waited at the airport in the familiar Bronco. Kyle and Gregg spent a few minutes loading baggage into the airplane in order to save time the next morning. Then they all piled into the vehicle, Gregg at the wheel., Karen in the front beside him. She leaned back with a grateful sigh.

"Tired?" Gregg asked.

"Not really. It's just good to have room to stretch and relax a little."

"You didn't relax during the flight?" Gregg asked. "I believe I noticed you sleeping at one point."

"All right. It wasn't so bad. I was just a little tense," Karen explained.

"So what else is new?" Gregg grumbled.

"Don't worry, Karen," Kelly put in. "You have nothing to do but relax this weekend. That's our mission. To see that you and Gregg relax." She shifted to sit behind Gregg and began massaging his shoulders. "He's getting old before his time," she murmured affectionately.

"Don't get him too relaxed yet," Kyle said. "He's still driving."

"You know," Gregg said, studying them in the rearview mirror, "if I didn't know better, I'd think you were trying to soften me up for something."

"Aw, come on!" Kelly and Kyle chorused simultaneously. Then Kelly sat back. She threw her brother a look and turned back to Gregg. "You know, this really isn't fair. We never have been able to put anything over on you."

"You forget how many years I've watched you try." Gregg's voice was tinged with amusement.

Kelly's sigh was eloquent.

"So, what gives?" Gregg asked after a moment. Suddenly he reached out and tapped the fuel gauge. "Do you know you're almost out of gas?" he frowned.

"Yeah, well, I was distracted," Kyle said reluctantly.

"Distracted?" Gregg repeated.

"I got a speeding ticket on the way to the airport," Kyle said in a rush.

"But it was really my fault," Kelly said, hurrying to his defense. "I was running late—"

"That I don't doubt," Gregg said. "But you aren't the one in danger of losing his license or insurance coverage." His eyes were inscrutable through the dark glasses as they studied Kyle in the mirror.

"Here's a gas station," Karen said, hoping to ease the strain by distracting Gregg.

He glanced at her and then put on the signal to turn off the road. Kelly and Kyle got out of the vehicle before Gregg could open his door.

Karen looked at Gregg and saw a smile playing around his mouth.

"What's so funny?" she asked.

"Just trying to remember what it's like to be a teenager and for my biggest worry to be a traffic ticket."

"I wonder if they know how lucky they are to have you," Karen mused.

"What makes you think they're so lucky?" he growled, glancing at her.

"I don't think they're lucky. I know they are." Karen held his gaze.

He reached for her hand. "It wasn't the easiest job I've had becoming an instant father to two teenagers." He moved his thumb in a circular motion across the back of her hand.

"I'm sure it wasn't. You've done a wonderful job." Karen had trouble thinking, much less speaking.

"I had a lot of help. Rock and Megan started them out right. And of course, I had Mom and Grandmother to help. They're good kids." He smiled.

Karen drew in her breath. "They're great kids." She wanted to trace her finger across the chiseled lips, softened now in remembrance.

He released her hand. "I'm glad you think so. Incidentally, they like you, too."

Before Karen could reply, Kelly and Kyle scrambled back into the Bronco.

"Let's go. I'm starving," Kyle announced.

"Me, too," Kelly echoed.

"By all means," Gregg agreed. "The last thing I want is either of you passing out from hunger."

"It's still the middle of the night!" Karen protested, reaching for the pillow to pull it over her head.

"Nonsense!" Kelly replied. "It's five already."

"So what's the rush? Aren't we supposed to be on vacation?" Karen mumbled.

"Gregg wants to be in the air by sunrise. We hope to make Telluride by mid-morning."

Karen groaned and sat up, still clinging to the remnants of a dream. As she came awake the images faded and she saw a fully dressed Kelly standing beside the bed.

"Is that how I should dress?" she asked, taking in Kelly's jeans and sweater.

"Dress warmly. It'll get pretty cold when we get over the mountains, even with a heater in the plane."

In the kitchen a few minutes later Karen helped Kelly make sandwiches and fill a thermos with coffee. Kyle checked a box of survival gear.

"Double K!" Gregg's voice thundered from the next room.

Kelly's eyes widened and she looked at Kyle. "Uncle Taz!" she whispered. As if by magic they both disappeared from the room, leaving Karen to look at Gregg with a bemused expression as he entered.

"Funny," she said, before he could speak. "I don't see any fangs or claws."

"What does that mean?" He poured a cup of coffee. "I thought the twins were in here."

"They were," Karen said. "Then you roared out *Double K*, Kelly gasped *Uncle Taz* and they both vanished. What is it about that expression that strikes terror in the hearts of nineteen-year-olds?" Her eyes and voice were teasing as she watched him.

Gregg smiled. "Rock started using the term Double K as soon as they began walking. They were always together and everywhere at the same time, it seemed. When they got into trouble, there was no way of knowing which one was the guilty party. He figured whatever one was up to, the other was at least guilty by association. That still seems to hold, kinda like Kyle getting a speeding ticket because Kelly was running late."

"So what have they done now?" Karen asked.

"Nothing that I'm aware of. They must have a guilty conscience."

"So why call out *Double K*?"

"Because I wanted them both. As they grew older, the expression simply became a way of calling both of them at the same time."

Karen studied him, decided he was being honest. "They disappeared through there," she said, turning back to the sandwiches.

Sunrise was spectacular, Karen decided, when viewed from a few thousand feet above the earth. Ever since the plane had lifted off into the cool crisp morning, she had not been able to keep her eyes off the scenery below. They would have to climb higher, Gregg had said, as they approached the mountains, but for now they were flying along at a little over a mile high. She felt Kelly watching her and turned from the window, a smile touching her lips.

"Do you ever get used to this view?" she asked.

Kelly grinned. "Some people don't. Gregg, for instance. Me? If you've seen one sunrise over the Rockies, you've seen them all." She leaned over to look past Karen. "Although I have to admit this one is rather spectacular." She settled back in her seat and Karen returned to staring enthralled at the view below.

Karen shifted her attention from the scenery to Gregg's profile. He wore his dark glasses and leather jacket. Kyle sat in the seat beside him and Karen could hear Gregg going over the fine points of mountain flying.

Gregg turned to look over his shoulder and Karen gave a little start. She could not see his expression because of his glasses, but she knew what he could see in her eyes. After a moment she relaxed and smiled. He immediately returned her smile.

"How about some coffee?" he asked.

"Are you sure you wouldn't like to try and get some sleep?" Kyle asked before Karen could reply.

Gregg glanced at Kyle and Karen saw his lips twitch. "With you at the controls? I believe I'll pass on sleep for the moment."

"Suit yourself," Kyle said, "but I'll need you more later when we're over the mountains."

"Don't worry. I'll be here. I'm not sleepy." He turned back, shifting comfortably in the seat, and Karen handed him the coffee she had poured during the exchange. "Thanks," he murmured. His hand brushed hers as he reached for the mug.

Karen could not take her eyes off his face. Smiling and relaxed, a dimple danced in his right cheek. She knew he must be able to read the yearning in her eyes, but she was powerless to look away.

"Are you glad you came?" Kelly asked Gregg. Karen saw Kelly's concern as she studied her uncle.

"Yes, Kitten." He reached back and caught her hand. "I'm glad I came. We really should do this more often."

"I wasn't sure we'd ever do it again!" Kelly whispered, her eyes suddenly sparkling with tears.

Karen looked from one to the other, a sudden premonition chilling her. "When—did you last go to Telluride?"

143

"Just before Mom was killed," Kyle said, turning his head briefly. "She died the next week."

Karen's eyes locked with Gregg's, although she couldn't see his through the dark lenses. Her lips parted and after a moment she moistened them nervously and turned back to the window.

"Karen, it's all right. We're fine." Gregg's voice gently reassured her. "Megan loved coming here. I wanted to share this with you."

She looked back at him, her eyes full of all that she felt. She heard him draw in his breath and saw him swallow. Then he raised the mug and drank, his eyes never leaving her face. She had trouble breathing.

"Can we go skiing tonight?" Kelly asked, effectively destroying the quiet intimacy. Karen drew a deep breath.

"Tonight?" Gregg looked at Kelly. "You mean this afternoon?"

"No. I mean tonight. This is Easter weekend. We have almost a full moon. Remember how beautiful the snow is in the moonlight?"

"That sounds like a perfect way to end the day," Karen said. "Seeing the sun come up from the air, then skiing under a full moon."

"Not you, too!" Gregg said in mock protest. "Sounds like I need to coin a new phrase. Triple K!"

Karen's eyes widened but before she had time to fully grasp the significance of this, Kyle turned in his seat to give her a high-five.

"Way to go, Karen!" he grinned.

"Welcome to the club!" Kelly said, putting her arm around Karen's shoulder in a quick hug.

Gregg groaned. "On second thought, maybe I've created a monster!"

CHAPTER THIRTEEN

The moon was well hidden, Gregg noted as he stood on the balcony of the ski lodge and frowned up at the dark rolling clouds. They had gotten in an afternoon of skiing. The sunset had been spectacular, but shortly after the weather had taken a turn for the worse. Not only would there be no skiing in the moonlight, there might not be any skiing the rest of the weekend. The temperature had to drop a few more degrees for the precipitation to fall as snow. If it fell as rain, it would wash away the existing snow.

Gregg leaned back against the railing and looked through the glass doors at the group gathered around the fireplace. His frown deepened. Karen had been surrounded by admirers from the moment of their arrival. He hadn't been able to get near her. Her natural beauty and easy grace drew men like a magnet. Kelly and Kyle hadn't left her side, either, apparently as enthralled with her as everyone else.

Come to think of it, Kelly attracted plenty of attention in her own right. Gregg's frown deepened even more. *When had she grown up?*

Gregg stiffened as Karen broke away from the group and walked toward the balcony. He held his breath as he saw her hesitate for a moment before pushing open the door. Then she stood beside him.

"Are you avoiding me?" Karen asked as she crossed over to the railing. "I didn't come up here to be abandoned to a pack of—pack of—" She sighed. "Actually, I guess they're nice enough. But I'm tired of refusing drinks and being offered cigarettes. I want—"

Gregg crossed the distance between them and drew her into his arms. Karen sighed in contentment as she nestled against him.

"Thank you," she whispered.

"Why did you come up here?" Gregg asked.

"For this." Her eyes held his as she laughed up at him.

He tipped her face up and bent his head.

"What are you doing?" Karen asked.

"Sniffing your breath. To see if you've had too much to drink."

"I haven't had anything to drink." She shivered. "No one has offered me hot cocoa."

He grinned. "My kind of date. Come on. I'll see if I can bribe someone into making some."

"What are you doing out here all alone?" Karen asked.

"Feeling sorry for myself. You've been surrounded by half the male patrons of the lodge since we arrived. I didn't know how I could possibly compete for your attention."

"And I've been wondering why you didn't come and rescue me from all that attention. Kyle finally whispered that you were out here and I managed to escape." She looked up at him, and Gregg realized that the moon had broken through the clouds, bathing her face in radiant light. "Don't abandon me again!" she pleaded.

"When you ask like that—" Gregg began, to break off as Karen slipped her arms around his neck and raised her face to his. His arms went around her to gather her against him. "I've been waiting for this," he whispered as his mouth found hers.

"You didn't have to," she said when she could speak. "I've been here."

"What do you say we go back to the cabin and make our own cocoa?" Gregg said, his eyes burning into hers.

"With a fire in the fireplace?"

"By all means."

"You have a deal."

Gregg pulled her protectively against his side and they crossed the balcony to go down the steps and across the snow to the row of cabins. He dug in his pocket for a key and pushed the door open.

Karen stepped inside and Gregg followed, closing the door behind him.

"I'll get the fire going if you'll start the cocoa," he said, valiantly resisting the urge to pull her into his arms again.

"Okay," Karen said after a moment of hesitation. "I guess that would be—yes, okay. I'll see what I can do." She turned toward the kitchen.

Gregg watched her go, wondering at her reluctance. Then he turned to the fire, already laid, and looked around for a match. In a few minutes the fire crackled and he removed his jacket.

Karen came in with a tray in time to see Gregg strip off his sweatshirt and toss it on a chair beside his jacket. He wore black jeans and a black and blue flannel shirt. As she watched he unfastened a couple of buttons near his throat and sighed in relief. She tore her gaze away.

Gregg turned as he heard Karen put the tray on a table near the fire. She straightened and unzipped her jacket.

"It warmed up quickly," she commented, tossing her jacket beside his.

"Didn't it?" Gregg barely recognized his voice. A butter yellow sweater of softest knit, well worn jeans, and short leather boots completed her outfit. Her hair was windblown and tangled from being tucked under a knit cap all day. He'd never seen a more beautiful woman.

"You found what you needed for cocoa?" Gregg looked at the tray.

"Yes." The silence stretched between them.

"How long are the twins planning to stay at the lodge?" Gregg moved to sit down. He reached for a mug and sipped the drink.

"A couple of hours. A band started warming up when I escaped."

"A band?" Gregg raised his brows. "You don't like music?"

"At nineteen, I could probably have listened to *Weird Charlie and the Lunatics*. My tastes have changed a bit over the years." She sat down on the sofa just out of his reach and picked up her cocoa.

Gregg frowned. Why should this be so hard when he wanted to say so much to her, and he finally had an opportunity to do so?

"I noticed that Kelly is growing up," Gregg said, not sounding too pleased at the thought.

"Growing up?" Karen looked at him. "I have news for you, Uncle Taz. She's grown up."

148

He shook his head. "She's still a child—"

"Has she told you about her boy friend?" Karen asked.

His head snapped up. "Boy friend?"

"It sounds fairly serious. He's an Israeli exchange student, and a Colonel in their air force. All she talks about is Josh this and Josh that—"

"Not to me, she doesn't," Gregg growled.

"Have you given her a chance?" Karen asked. "She worships you, you know?"

Gregg relaxed, leaned back and looked at her. "And why shouldn't she?" he demanded, his eyes laughing, his voice light and teasing.

"No reason." Karen matched his tone. "If I was nineteen and had an uncle like you, I'd probably be rather crazy about him, too."

In a heartbeat, Gregg's mood changed. He stretched his arm along the back of the sofa and caught a tendril of hair to twine around his finger. "I'm more interested in how a certain thirty-year-old who's no relation at all feels about me."

Karen's hand shook and she put down her mug before she spilled the contents. "Not until Monday," she said.

"I beg your pardon?"

"I won't be thirty until Monday," she said. "Let's not rush these things. Oh, and according to Angela, we are related—distantly."

"How distant?" Gregg asked.

"Well, it seems that Rodney McClaren—"

"My grandfather," Gregg said.

"—and Stanley McGraw—"

"Your grandfather."

"Yes. Their mothers were sisters. They had maternal grandparents in common."

"Which would have been—what? Our great-great-grandparents. I don't think that's close enough."

"Close enough for what?"

"For us to be considered blood relations."

"Um. Too bad. Having you for a cousin might not—"

"I don't think it's too bad. Especially since I have a different relationship in mind." His hand tangled in the hair at the back of her neck and he turned her toward him. "Karen, will you marry me? Right away. As soon as we can make the arrangements. I don't think—I can't go on without you." As she stared at him, breath suspended, he shook her gently. "Please say something," he pleaded. "Anything—except no."

Karen stared at Gregg as a hundred little rockets seemed to explode inside her head. *Had she heard right?* Had he asked her to marry him? She shook her head to clear it.

Gregg drew a ragged breath. "Please don't say no," he whispered. He cradled her face in his hands and she felt them tremble.

She wet her lips. "I—did I hear right? Did you ask me to marry you?"

He nodded, his eyes never leaving hers.

"Why?" she whispered, her eyes wide in wonder.

"Because I need you. I want you. *We're good together.*" He broke off and his eyes narrowed on her face. "And because I love you." He stood up and pulled her into his arms, crushing her against him. "Oh, God, how I love you!" He rained tiny kisses over her face, her eyelids.

"But—" Karen tried to think coherently. "But there's so many things you don't know about me—about us—" she protested weakly.

"Please say you'll marry me."

"I—" Karen turned away to begin pacing. "I don't know if I can." She stopped to look at him. "There are too many things standing in the way."

"Things such as?"

"My job. My inheritance."

"Why are they problems?"

"I thought I could walk away from my inheritance, but you pointed out that there are others involved that I could help—perhaps even Amanda." She paused. "And my job. I still have one more story to write. By the time I return I should have all the information I need to see that Dr. Fumara never practices medicine in this country again." She watched his face as she spoke.

Gregg kept his feelings carefully masked, knowing she expected him to react, to protest. "Have you considered any of the positive aspects of marrying me?" he asked instead.

The question caught her by surprise and she smiled slightly. "Other than the obvious, I guess I haven't," she admitted.

"We could adopt Michael and Amanda."

She stared at him, her breath catching softly. Then, "That's blackmail!"

"Of course it is. And I'm just getting started. I'm an expert at getting what I want." His eyes smiled at her, his voice teased.

"And you want me?" Karen asked in wonder.

"More than I've ever wanted anything."

"And when did you decide this?" She didn't look convinced.

He went to stand before the fire. "I think I've known it from the beginning, ever since I took that 9-1-1 call and found you holding off a gang of teenage thugs with a can of hairspray."

Karen shivered involuntarily as she remembered.

"I finally admitted it a couple of weeks ago when I saw you again in the park," he went on. "And I decided to do something about it a few days ago when you wouldn't listen to reason, and I had to kiss you to get your attention."

"To get my attention—" Karen broke off to stare at him. She pressed her lips together. "Well, you did that," she said, her voice almost a whisper. "I haven't thought of much else since that kiss."

"So, how about it?"

"How about what?"

"Marrying me," he replied with exaggerated patience.

She sighed. "I don't know, Gregg." Her eyes sought his, troubled, uncertain. "Can you understand? I don't know." She began pacing again. "I've never even dated, not really. Never more than once with the same guy." She gave a short, self-derisive laugh. "The last time was at least two years ago."

"What happened then?" Gregg asked.

She glanced at him. "Are you sure you want to know?"

"No, but tell me anyway."

"I had been working with our legal department on a story and one of the lawyers asked me out. The first time I turned him down. It's too bad I didn't pay more attention to my own instincts." She sat down again, her hands clasped between her knees.

"He asked a couple more times and I finally agreed to go to dinner and a play. Everything went along pleasantly enough until time to go home. He

152

turned to me with a totally straight face and asked, '*Okay, sweetheart, which will it be? Your place or mine?*'"

Gregg's mouth twisted. "That subtle, huh?"

Karen shrugged. "I'll admit to being stunned. So I said in the coldest voice I could manage, 'How about both? You go to yours—' He then proceeded to explain that he had made a considerable investment in the evening and he expected a return on that investment."

"So what did you do?"

"I got out of the car, politely invited him to send me a bill, then walked across the street and called a cab."

"Did he send you a bill?"

"I didn't give him a chance. I know how to get information. I called the ticket agency and the restaurant, got the amount of the bills to the penny, typed up an itemized statement and sent him a check."

"Did he cash it?"

"Oh, yes. And that was the last bit of humiliation I was willing to subject myself to. Except for you, that is." She looked at him. "After all we've been through, do you realize we've never even had a proper date?"

"We haven't?"

"No. We worked together to identify two kids. We had two cases of breaking and entering, one vandalism, one attempted murder—"

"What do you call last weekend at the ranch?"

"We worked on the case—"

"You believe that?"

"Why wouldn't I? That's why you asked me to come—"

"I asked you to come because I couldn't stand the thought of not being with you. I wanted to get you away from the city so you could relax—"

"I don't know how to relax," Karen murmured.

"So I've noticed." He crossed to the sofa and sat down beside her. "Turn around."

She looked at him. "I beg your pardon?"

"I'm going to rub your neck and shoulders," he said. "You *will* relax."

She looked skeptical. "Is this a good idea?"

"It's a great idea." He turned her again, positioning her, and then he began massaging her neck and shoulders.

"Mmmmmmm," Karen murmured blissfully. "That does feel good!" He continued to work on the knotted muscles in her neck.

"Ouch!"

"Relax!"

She leaned against him, her shoulders against his chest, and after a moment Gregg slipped his arms around her. "That's enough for a first session." He buried his face against her neck.

"Gregg?"

"Ummmm?"

"I don't know if I can marry you. Can you understand at all? I need some time."

He sighed. "I'll try to be patient. At least for a couple of days." Before she could protest his arms tightened to cradle her with infinite tenderness, his head bent over hers.

Unwilling to think anymore, and unable to do so in the circle of his arms, Karen relaxed against his chest, closing her eyes blissfully. Her hands rested on top of his. At last she stirred and turned to look up at him speculatively.

"You know, that really is a powerful argument," she said, "and you don't play fair."

"I beg your pardon?" But his eyes were amused.

She turned toward him, played with a button on his shirt. "Holding me in your arms, silently showing me all I'll miss if I don't agree to marry you. Pretty sneaky, if you ask me."

"I could show you more, if you're interested."

Karen felt herself drowning in the laughing depths of his eyes. How she had wanted to see him relax! To laugh. To smile. She traced his lips with a fingertip.

"Perhaps you should," she whispered. "Possibly I've forgotten a thing or two—"

The door burst open at that moment and Kyle and Kelly spilled into the room. Karen let her hands drop and moved away from Gregg, but not before she saw the response and the promise in his eyes.

"It's snowing like crazy!" Kelly said. "A couple of inches have fallen already." Then, "Oh, good! Cocoa." She picked up a mug from the tray and drank deeply. Her eyes widened and she choked. "This stuff is ice cold! What have you two been doing?" she asked in disgust.

Kyle ruffled her hair with an affectionate laugh. "My little sister! She still doesn't realize there are things in life preferable to hot cocoa." He picked up the tray. "Come on. We'll make some more."

As they left the room Karen glanced at Gregg to find him laughing silently. She let her own mirth erupt and collapsed against him to feel his arms close around her.

"I thought you said she was grown up," Gregg said, rubbing his chin against the top of her head.

"Well, maybe not as much as I thought," Karen admitted. "Although, she does have a point. Hot cocoa rates pretty high on my list of the good things in life, too."

Gregg sat up. "Shall we go help them make it?"

"I think we'd better."

CHAPTER FOURTEEN

Kyle looked up as they entered the kitchen. "Hey, they're having a slalom race tomorrow," he announced. "I think I'll enter."

Karen felt her body tense.

"There will be prizes for best male, female, under twelve and over seventy." Kyle explained, all the while watching Gregg.

Gregg frowned. "Have you at least thought about this?"

"I have. Do you realize this may be the last time I have a chance to go skiing? Especially with my family. All of us together like this."

"You have a point." Gregg's frown deepened. "Be careful, will you?"

"You aren't going to forbid me to do it?" Kyle asked in amazement.

"It has been pointed out to me that you and Kelly are grown up now. I trust that means you have acquired some degree of common sense. Also, you are the only one who really knows how much a career in the air force means to you, and whether or not you're willing to sacrifice it for a moment of glory on the ski slopes."

Kyle stared at him. "I hate it when you're logical!" he said in disgust.

Gregg laughed. "I'm merely returning the responsibility for the decision where it belongs. With you. I know that you're a good skier. But I also know the chances you take. Maybe this is a litmus test for the air force. If you are undisciplined enough to injure yourself by taking foolish chances, you probably aren't cut out for the job, anyway."

Two pairs of blue eyes locked in a battle of wills. Gregg's cool and appraising. Kyle's wary.

"I'll think about it," Kyle agreed at last.

Gregg grinned and clapped him on the shoulder. "That's all I'm asking."

"Anyone for hot cocoa?" Kelly asked. "I even found some marshmallows."

"Now that's the kind of offer I've been waiting for," Gregg grinned.

Kelly looked at Karen, her eyes questioning. "How about you, Karen?"

She shook her head. "I think I've had my limit." She turned away, her expression concerned. *How could she stop Kyle from possibly making the same mistake she had made at his age?*

"Who is that?" The judge at the bottom of the slope jerked his head up and stared at Karen as she came out of the gate and began her slalom run.

Gregg looked at the man and back at Karen. He easily picked out her purple and yellow ski suit. Whatever she had in mind, she had asked that he and Kelly and Kyle wait for her at the finish line.

"Number Five," the judge went on. He checked the clipboard in his hands, a frown creasing his brow. "I'd recognize that style anywhere. Must be a late entry. I don't have a name yet."

"Her name is Karen--"

"Karen McGraw!" the judge thundered, looking at Gregg. "Where has she been for the last twelve years?"

"What are you talking about?" Gregg asked.

"Karen McGraw was the hottest number on the skiing circuit when she was eighteen. She made the Olympic team. I was her coach. Then, the first day of training, she broke her leg. I haven't heard from her since." He glanced back at the figure flying down the slope. "But it doesn't look as if she's lost much over the years!" His voice and expression were filled with admiration and respect.

Gregg looked at Kyle to see that his face had paled. Gregg's mouth tightened. Now he knew what Karen intended to do. He turned back to watch her progress. Grace and skill and perfection, she attacked the slope with a speed no one could maintain. All eyes riveted on her as she zigzagged down the slope. He heard gasps of awe and horror in turn as she narrowly missed hitting post after post. Time seemed to stand still, as he waited, heart pounding, for her to make it past the last one.

The judge groaned. "She's going to do it again!" Then a collective sigh of relief as she made it through the last gate still on her feet.

Karen crossed the finish line and skied in a large graceful circle to slow her speed, sending up a spray of snow. Her lungs burned and every muscle in her body cried out in protest. She would pay dearly for this little demonstration, she knew. Already her leg ached, above and beyond all the other pain she felt. Well, she rationalized, unless she could prove to Kyle how good she'd been, how could she impress upon him how much a careless injury had cost her when she had been his age?

Coasting to a stop, Karen looked up to see a crowd descending upon her. She recognized Gregg's navy and red ski suit and Kelly and Kyle's matching green ones. The man with the judge's vest—Cappy. She smiled.

"Karen!" The burly man enfolded her in his arms. "Where have you been? That was quite a run for someone who hasn't skied competitively for twelve years."

"How do you know—" Karen began.

"If you had, I would've known. I tried to find out what happened to you. I knew the break was bad, but I thought you might stay with the sport. Become a coach yourself, maybe. You were such a natural."

Karen shook her head. "Then you should understand why I had to make a complete break from skiing. Being a groupie has-been wasn't for me."

"I guess not." Cappy still held her hand. "Can we talk later? I have to finish this race—although I think it's over," he added dryly.

Karen smiled. "It's good to see you again, Cappy, but I don't think we have anything to talk about. Find some reason to disqualify me so someone else can win. I've already done what I needed to do." She gave him a last quick hug and turned away.

She reached down to release her skies and step out of them, then looked up to meet Gregg's eyes. Not liking what she saw, she glanced at Kyle, took in his pale strained face. He gave her a terse nod. She nodded in reply.

She looked back at Gregg, her eyes pleading for understanding. His mouth tightened.

160

"I'm wondering what else you might still have to spring on me", he growled. "Would it have been too much for you to let us in on this escapade?"

Karen grimaced. "I don't suppose you'd believe I really didn't plan this. It's just that when I came out of the gate—" Her eyes went to Cappy, still standing there.

He nodded. "I understand. You never got to finish that last run."

Her eyes flooded with tears and she turned away. She bent down to gather up her skis.

Someone touched her and she straightened. The arms that went around her were not Gregg's, but Kyle drew her close for a hug. Then he rested his forehead against hers.

"I know why you did what you did," he said. "And I want to say thanks. You're the greatest."

"Once maybe," Karen tried to joke. Then she put her hands on his arms. "For you, no problem."

Kyle nodded with an understanding far beyond his nineteen years. Karen's heart swelled with love for this wonderful young man. Then she released him and turned to find Kelly beside her, face streaked with tears.

"I've never been so frightened," Kelly sobbed, throwing her arms around Karen. "But you were perfect."

"Kelly!" Karen gasped, feeling that her heart had been clamped in a vise. "I never thought—I would never have frightened you. Please believe that!" Kelly had had enough fright and loss already to last a lifetime. Karen had had no intention of adding to it.

Kyle gently disengaged Kelly's arms from around Karen and put his arm around her to lead her aside and try and comfort her. Karen looked after them, reluctant to turn and face Gregg and the disappointment she had seen in his eyes.

Gregg looked from Kelly to Karen, indecision battering him. Kelly had Kyle, but she had always known she had him, too. He turned abruptly and made his way over to his niece and nephew.

Gregg waited outside the infirmary with Kyle while Kelly went inside to look for Karen. When he had glanced around after Kelly's outburst, Karen was no where to be found. After a few words with her former coach, they had set off to search for her.

"Karen's special, isn't she?" Kyle asked. He hadn't spoken to Gregg since Karen's dramatic run down the slope.

"Special in what way?" Gregg pulled himself back to look at Kyle.

"Well, first of all, to you. Isn't she?"

Gregg smiled. "I guess you could say that. I've asked her to marry me, if that tells you anything."

Kyle grinned. "Wow! That's great—"

"She hasn't said yes," Gregg added dryly.

"She will," Kyle predicted. "How could she not?"

"What does that mean?"

"Well, look what she risked to prove a point to someone as undeserving as me—"

Gregg's head jerked around. "What do you mean? Prove what point?"

Kyle stared at his boots. "She could have just told me what happened to her. Do you think that would have made much of an impression?"

"I doubt it."

"So she had to prove to me just how good she'd been before she lost it all to an accident. She was the best and still something went wrong. So where do I get off thinking it couldn't happen to me?" Kyle studied his feet for a moment longer then raised his head to meet Gregg's eyes. He looked disgusted with himself.

Gregg stared at him, thankful that Karen's lesson had reached home.

Kyle cleared his throat. "Anyway, as I was saying. You deserve her. Or at least you would if you let up a little. If you weren't so hard on her."

"Hard on her?" Gregg stared at him. "She scared me half to death. I didn't mean to be so hard on her."

"I think she could probably use a little understanding right now," Kyle suggested.

Gregg's mouth tightened as he glared at his nephew. Then his mouth twitched. "Thanks. I'll take your advice under consideration."

Kyle grinned. "Anytime. Always glad to help."

Gregg turned as the door opened. Kelly stormed out of the office.

"She didn't come here!"

Gregg's heart thudded.

"Do you think she's back at the cabin?" Kyle asked.

"Where else could she be?" Kelly asked. "But why would she go back there alone?"

Gregg was afraid he knew only too well why she would go back to the cabin alone.

Karen stilled, sensed someone behind her, and turned to see Gregg filling the doorway. The jolt of her heart vibrated through her whole body.

His glance fell to the duffel bag she had packed. "Going somewhere?"

She nodded, not looking at him. "I have a ride to the airport at noon. A commuter flight leaves at two."

"Just like that?"

She looked at him then. "What are you asking me?"

He didn't answer that question, asked one of his own.

"How is your leg? How badly did you injure it?"

"What makes you think I injured it?" she asked nonchalantly.

"I talked to your coach. I know all about the broken leg ten years ago."

"I didn't injure it. It just isn't as strong as it used to be, and certainly not strong enough to do what I asked of it back there."

"Multiple compound breaks, Karen," Gregg reminded her. "You don't have to act tough for me. There might be some people you could fool, but I'm not one of them. Cappy said it was a miracle they saved your leg."

Exhausted, in excruciating pain, and close to tears, Karen sat down on the bed. She met his eyes. "I don't want to ruin this trip, Gregg. It's important to the twins, important to you as a family. I'm an outsider—"

"You can't possibly believe that. Have we done such a poor job of making you feel you belong?"

She squeezed her eyes tight over the tears. "It isn't that. You don't need me. You don't need the baggage that keeps cropping up at every turn."

"Are you thinking about me—or about yourself?" Gregg asked, his voice bitter now, accusing.

She looked at him, shook her head. "What are you talking about?"

"Maybe it's my problems you don't want to deal with," he suggested icily. "I've been there before. I'm well aware that I come with a full compliment of what you term baggage. Let's at least be honest—"

"No!" Karen gasped. "That's not it at all. I love the twins. I love your grandmother."

"Do you love me?"

Her head jerked up and she stared at him. She wet her lips. "I've already told you—"

"You threw out once that in spite of all the cruel and thoughtless things I've done and said, you still managed to fall in love with me. I don't remember ever hearing the actual words, *'I love you, Gregg'.*"

Karen tried to stand, to pace. Pain shot through the calf of her leg and she sank back.

"I guess I haven't said them because until last night, I had no idea how you felt about commitment. I thought this was all one-sided. Your asking me to marry you was the last thing I expected."

His eyes flickered and went cold. "And you don't believe I really meant it?" he guessed.

She did not meet his eyes.

"You once told me that you didn't think I'd ever said anything I didn't mean," he reminded her.

Karen closed her eyes. Swallowed. "I'm sorry, Gregg. It's very hard to believe that someone could really, truly love me, when I don't love myself." She swallowed again and when she spoke her words were barely a whisper. "And when the most important person in my life couldn't love me."

Gregg looked down at her, his heart twisting.

God, give me the right words to say. Show me what to do.

Then he remembered Kyle's words. *"I think she could probably use a little understanding right now."* Kyle also felt he was too hard on her.

He crossed over to kneel in front of her, to catch the hands clasped in her lap. He pried them apart, felt their trembling, and brought them together inside his own.

"I'm sorry, my love."

As he watched, she lost the battle against her tears and huge drops began rolling down her face.

"When you turned away from me at the finish line, I've never felt so alone in my life," she gulped between sobs. "Except that first time—"

The area around his heart tightened painfully. He had read the plea for understanding in her eyes and chosen to ignore it. She had put herself at great risk and through excruciating pain for Kyle's sake, and he had turned his back on her. Could she forgive him? Could he forgive himself?

"I'm sorry," he said again. He reached to pull her to her feet.

Karen cried out in pain.

"What's wrong?" Gregg stared at her.

She sank back on the bed. "I can't even stand, let alone walk."

Gregg swung her up into his arms. "So much for your ride to the airport and that commuter flight."

"What are you doing?"

"Taking you to the infirmary as I should have done an hour ago. And then we're going to talk! I have a lot of explaining to do."

Karen lay on the sofa, feeling as if every bone in her body had melted. Cappy had insisted she spend an hour in the whirlpool and then treated her to one of his '*killer*' massages. Reluctantly, she agreed to take the pain reliever Cappy had sent with Gregg. Now she could hear Gregg puttering around in the kitchen as he prepared lunch.

He'd said they would talk. About what? she wondered. The past between their first meeting when he rescued her from a gang of teenage thugs to their encounter in the park beside the two white crosses? That past had been filled with bitter clashes that always left Karen feeling small and insignificant.

From the first she had been drawn to Gregg. She watched from her vantage point on the roof as he dispersed the young ruffians. He then told her to come down. To her horror, she found that her legs refused to obey her commands. He apparently sensed what was happening because he climbed the ladder and held a hand out to her. She then managed, with his help, to regain the ground. Once there, however, her legs threatened to fail her again.

She wanted to throw herself into his arms, to draw from his strength. Tears pressed behind her eyelids and her lips trembled. Through a blur of emotion, she'd seen his eyes darken, felt his hands tighten on her arms. Then he began berating her unmercifully for her stupidity and carelessness in getting herself into such a situation.

Anger burned away the numbness that had overtaken her. She pulled away from him, pride lending her strength as she straightened her shoulders and tried to collect her scattered wits. Flippantly, she thanked him for his chivalry and his concern, then turned and walked away, jaw set and head high.

What could they talk about? she wondered. They had clashed from the first moment. How could she believe anything had changed? *Would change?*

Gregg came in carrying a tray and placed it on a table within her reach. "Soup and sandwiches," he announced. "Just what the doctor ordered. Well, Cappy, at least."

Karen shifted to a sitting position. "Something smells wonderful." Her eyes widened. "Pastrami on rye?" She sounded awe struck. "I know I didn't tell Kelly that's my favorite sandwich."

"No? I took a chance. It happens to be mine." He reached for one and took a bite, his eyes closing in appreciation.

Karen studied him. Relaxed and happy as he seemed to be now, she would never recognize the uptight, thin lipped police officer who had plagued her days and haunted her nights off and on for the better part of six years.

Gregg opened his eyes and caught her expression. "What are you thinking?"

She shook her head. "I'm thinking how different you are now from the Gregg Watson who rescued me and then bullied me for all those years. You said we would talk—"

He winced. "Yes. We have to. Because I can see that I'm going to lose you if I don't explain—try and redeem myself."

"Gregg—" Her voice was troubled. Was she really ready to hear his explanations?

"No, let me talk." He put down his sandwich.

"Please." She put her hand over his. "Let's eat first. You went to all the trouble to prepare lunch. Let's—not ruin things, yet."

He took her hand and brought it to his lips. "I don't intend to ruin things." He brushed his lips across her knuckles. "I want to explain that I never intended to hurt you." He sighed and released her hand. "Lunch first."

After they had eaten in silence for a few moments, Gregg leaned back. "You never told me. Why did you decide to become a reporter?"

"Actually, I didn't." Her eyes sparked with mischief. "I became a journalist."

He raised his brows. "My mistake."

She shrugged. "I became interested when I read about this wonderful lady named Lydia Marshall from Crandall, New Mexico—"

Gregg made a choking sound and Karen broke off to look at him. He stared at her. She watched as he put his sandwich down again.

"Are you telling me you know Lydia Marshall?" he asked, stunned.

"Well, yes. I got to meet her when I received my scholarship. You see, my mother wouldn't pay for me to go to college, unless I majored in fine arts or modeling, or something useless—" She broke off. "Anyway, Lydia became my role model. She invited me to visit her in New Mexico. I fell in love with Crandall and the people there."

"I can understand that," Gregg said, his voice carefully controlled.

Karen looked at him again, remembering. "That's right. You've been to Crandall. You know Lori and Bryan."

"Bryan Marshall is one of my best friends. But just how do you happen to know that?"

"Three years ago Lydia had me do a story on the Children's Center that Lori and Jill started. I got to know Lori then. Of course, I've known Bryan for years. He's the brother I never had. They got married a couple of years ago. They helped restore my faith in happy endings. Of course, no one deserves happiness more than they do, especially Lori."

"Amen to that," Gregg said huskily. "But I still can't believe we both know—" He shrugged. "Of course. Your connection was journalism. Lydia's family owns half the newspapers in the Southwest."

"And your connection?" Karen drew in her breath. "Bryan and his father are both police officers. That's how you met?"

"Sort of. My father and Frank Marshall were old war buddies. After Megan and Rock were married, I found myself at a loss. It's hard to learn to be an individual when you grow up a twin. Dad sent me out to stay with Frank for awhile and go through the police academy with Bryan. I didn't particularly need a role model. Dad filled that role just fine. But I really respected Frank. Then, less than a year later, I lost Dad. Frank stepped in and the Marshalls became a second family to me. Anytime I needed to get away I knew they were there."

"That's how I felt," Karen said, "especially since I didn't have such a good relationship with my mother. Lydia encouraged me, gave me references. I—it would have been a lot harder without her support." She blinked at the tears that stung her eyes.

"Which brings us back to my part in making your life even more difficult," Gregg said with a heavy sigh.

Karen shook her head. "I'm not sure you're that much at fault. If I had been a bit more hardened—"

"My only excuse is that I was as scared as you were after I chased those hoodlums away. I feared they might come back, once they realized I was alone. You began trembling and I thought you were either going to go into hysterics—or faint. If I had to deal with you and they did come back—" He drew a shuddering breath.

"Aren't you supposed to slap people when they go into hysterics?" Karen asked flatly.

"I had already rejected that. There is no way I could have slapped you.

Then I remembered Frank explaining to me how sustaining an emotion anger is. I thought if I made you angry, you'd be able to pull yourself together, at least long enough for me to get you to safety."

"So you decided to destroy me," Karen said. "I would rather have been slapped."

"No! I didn't intend to be quite so harsh. I told you that situation was as close to Hell as I ever hope to get. I started to get angry, too, that you would put yourself at such risk."

"I know. You made that very clear."

He sighed. "I had no idea how effective my tactics would be. You walked away like a conquering empress. A few days later I stopped by the Clarion, hoping to talk to you and try to explain. They told me you were on assignment. I figured you hadn't suffered any permanent damage from either experience if you were already back at work."

"But I wasn't. I asked for a couple weeks leave and flew out to cry on Lydia's shoulder. I came very close to quitting journalism. Not because I was afraid, but because you destroyed something that made me who I was. I never regained it. Years earlier I had found myself as a reporter. Now I had to start over and rebuild everything."

"I'm sorry—"

"Don't be. I think I built better the second time around. I liked myself a lot better. Lydia helped me regain my confidence—suggested I might change my approach to reporting. I should probably thank you—"

"And all the other times?" Gregg asked.

"I don't think they were your fault. I never gave you a chance after that. I always attacked first, to try and gain an advantage. I would hate myself afterwards, but it was the only way I knew to keep you from hurting me again."

171

She sighed. "In the end, it didn't seem to matter." Her lips trembled. "I still fell in love with you—even believing you hated me."

Gregg shook his head. "I never hated you—or your job. I had never felt so drawn to anyone. You were so attractive and brilliant. Everyone else liked you. Jack's crazy about you. I knew I was wrong, but I couldn't find a way to make things right between us, until I saw you at the crosses."

"I had just talked to my lawyer after I found out about the clause my mother put in the will. The money didn't matter, but knowing she still wanted to control my life—" She blinked. "Seeing the crosses was too much."

Gregg touched her arm. "I'm sorry, darling. So sorry you didn't have a mother you loved—"

She raised tear drenched eyes to his. "I don't believe I've ever said I didn't love my mother. My mother—never loved me—" She pressed a slender hand to her mouth as her voice broke.

She felt herself being enfolded in Gregg's arms and surrendered to the strength and security surrounding her.

"It's okay, sweetheart!" Gregg murmured.

She clung to him. "This is what I wanted the day you rescued me!"

"The hardest thing I've ever done was keep from pulling you into my arms that day. I wanted to protect you—take care of you—never let anything threaten or frighten you again." A sigh shook him, and he gathered her closer. "I pray for a chance to make all that up to you!"

CHAPTER FIFTEEN

"So much for a second chance!" Gregg muttered. He crushed the note he found propped against the coffeemaker and threw it across the room.

He knew better than to leave Karen alone while he drove his mother and grandmother back to the ranch. She had been entirely too quite since they returned from the skiing trip, and now she was gone. *Back to Kansas.* To her legacy. To everything that had brought her hurt and sadness her entire life.

As if you didn't cause a major share of that hurt, yourself, an inner voice mocked.

But he had apologized, begged for another chance. He crossed the room to retrieve the note and smoothed it again. She didn't mention coming back. Just said as things were now, she wasn't any good for either of them. *She wasn't what he needed.*

"You're so wrong, my love!" Gregg closed his eyes, squeezed the lids together tightly and swallowed.

Dear God, please bring her back. Let her find whatever it is that's missing in her life and realize that it's been right here all along.

Listlessly, Gregg crossed to the refrigerator, wondering if there would be anything edible inside. Then he sagged against the door and stared. Apparently Karen had completely restocked it for him. Pastrami, cheese, bread, eggs, milk, orange juice.

He pulled open the freezer section to see an assortment of frozen dinners and pastries, even a carton of Rocky Road ice cream. How had she known that?

The cupboards contained cans of soup and a couple of kinds of crackers, a box of cookies, and cereal.

He leaned back against the counter trying to figure out what this meant. Did it mean Karen cared for him and wanted to see that he ate properly? Or was this gesture merely to square things with her conscience.

This is a test, he told himself. You can be what she wants you to be by believing the first. Or your old cynical self can snag onto the second choice.

His stomach growled, reminding him not to look a gift horse in the mouth. He took out a frozen dinner, scanned the cooking instructions and ripped open the carton. The phone rang as he programmed the microwave.

Gregg reached for the receiver and tucked it under his chin.

"Hello?"

"How's the best cop in Colorado?"

His mind went on fast rewind as he tried to place the voice, then he felt a grin tilt his mouth. He dropped into a chair, leaning his arms on the table.

"Lori! I'm—fine. And how's the prettiest doctor in New Mexico?"

"Exhausted. Abandoned. Needing to hear a friendly voice," came the amused reply.

"Let me guess." He did a rapid mental calculation. "Jimmy is walking now and running you ragged. The abandoned part I don't get. Where's your worthless husband?"

She gave him an indirect answer. "Frank decided to retire."

Gregg let that sink in for a moment. "So that means Bryan will become police chief. But come on, Lori! In Crandall? He can't be that busy!"

"You'd be surprised. We're growing out here by hops and skips. We had ten new families move in last year."

Gregg whistled. "That many, huh. And I guess that's a boon for your business, too."

"Couple of new babies. Couple of broken arms. Mostly they came here because of Jill's clinic, then fell in love with the area and stayed."

"I can understand that," Gregg said.

She made a sound of disbelief. "With that ranch of yours? You have to be kidding. That has to be the most beautiful place on earth."

"Sure," he grumbled. "And if I get lucky, I see it maybe every other weekend."

"And whose choice is that, pray tell? You should have quit your job years ago, Gregg."

"Yeah, right." His shoulder twitched. "The twins are in college now. What's there for me?"

"Have it your way," Lori said. "I just want you to be happy, Gregg. You mean a lot to me."

175

He cleared his throat. "Same here."

"I'm glad."

"Do you think Bryan has any idea how lucky he is?"

An easy laugh. "You'll have to ask him some time." A pause. "By the way, I talked to a friend of yours a little while ago."

Gregg shook his head, drawing a blank. "Who? Steve? Walter?"

"Karen McGraw."

Gregg felt the silence stretching across two states. *Total and absolute.*

"Gregg?" Lori's voice questioned. "Did you hear me?"

He sighed. "I heard you, Lori." His voice sounded heavy and defeated and he couldn't do anything about it. "I just found out a few days ago that she knows everyone in Crandall."

"We became friends the same time I met you," Lori explained. "In fact, she mentioned you then."

He sat up. "She did?" Then he slumped in the chair again. "Well, it was obviously just a passing interest. She's gone now."

"But she'll come back."

"I can't let myself believe that." He dropped his forehead into his hand, elbow on the table. "No one else has."

"Gregg, please trust her," Lori pleaded.

His mouth tightened. "Did she ask you to call me?"

"Not at all. She just sounded so miserable and I wondered if you felt as bad as she does. I thought I would call and find out."

"Don't worry about me," Gregg said. "And if she's miserable, it is entirely her choice."

"Don't be so hard on her, Gregg."

He sighed. "Seems I've heard that before," he drawled. "Why did she leave, Lori? Did she tell you that?"

"She had to do this, Gregg."

He snorted.

"She has to find out if there is anyone, anywhere, who cares about her."

"Meaning I don't count—"

"You count more than anyone, but until Karen can make peace with her past, she can't accept that you care for her. In her mind, she isn't loveable."

"Unfortunately, over the years, I haven't done anything to help my cause," Gregg said heavily.

"We all make mistakes." Lori tried to console him.

"Me more than most," he said.

"She'll forgive you. Now you have to forgive yourself and move on."

"Move on?"

"Decide what, besides Karen, will make you happy for the rest of your life. So that when she comes back, she won't have any excuse not to stay."

"What are you talking about?" Gregg frowned.

"You're a bright boy, Gregg. You figure it out! And just to make sure you get it right, I'll send up a prayer or two on your behalf."

"You do that," he said. "I can use all the help I can get right now."

"Gregg," Lori hesitated, sighed. "Karen loves you. Whether she knows it or not, whether you know it or not, I've known it for three years."

Gregg was silent.

"What I'm trying to say is make it easy for Karen to come back. The longer she is away, the more doubt she will have that you still want her. You have to remove that doubt. She has the right key, Gregg."

"The right key?"

"The key that will unlock the door to that frozen fortress you've built around your heart. You just have to let her get close enough to use it." A pause. "Doctor's orders," Lori said firmly.

Gregg straightened. "Yes, doctor." Then, "Thanks for calling, Lori. Give Jimmy a big hug from *'Uncle Geggy'*, and tell Bryan 'Hi'."

"Oh, I might just give him a hug, too. That is, if I see him anytime soon," she grumbled.

Gregg grinned. "Take care, Lori."

"You, too."

Karen tore her gaze away from the view outside the window and turned back to the man behind the desk. Phillip Vaughn polished his reading glasses before settling them back on his nose.

"So you're telling me," she swallowed before going on, "that the moment I turned thirty, all the money became mine."

"That is the essence of your father's will. Your mother was caretaker of his estate until you reached thirty. Everything left is now yours."

"But I don't understand. Her will—"

Phillip shook his head. "I was your father's lawyer and I saw to it that your mother had plenty of money for her lifestyle and your care. Since everything she had was purchased with money from the estate, it all goes back into the estate. I have no idea why she felt a need to leave a will."

Karen swallowed again. "Her lawyer gave me a copy at the funeral. I assumed it to be legitimate. It even sounded like something she would do."

Again, he shook his head. "It has no bearing on your future, my dear."

"Are there any clauses in my father's will?" Karen asked. "Anything I am prohibited from doing or being?" She still felt the bitterness of her mother's last manipulation.

"He left a letter for you." He reached in a drawer and pulled out an envelope and handed it to her. "If there are any restrictions, they are only his wishes and therefore unenforceable. I can't imagine his making any unreasonable requests. Jason McGraw was the finest man I've ever known. You only need to sign a couple of papers and everything that's left will be yours, free and clear."

She looked at him. "Are the papers ready?"

"I can have Jean bring them in."

Karen shook her head. "I need to think about this. Can I come back in a couple of days? I will want to set up several trusts. And do you happen to know a good adoption lawyer?"

"I have some contacts, yes."

"Find the best one you know and set up an appointment for me. You can leave a message at home."

Karen drove to the house where she'd been born and subsequently spent small increments of her life. How different might things have been had she known her father? Everyone who knew Jason McGraw seemed to have admired him. As far as she knew, Karen had never even seen a picture of him. That was about to change. As soon as she had read his letter, she would search the house for scrapbooks, anything that might contain a photo.

Inside she took off her jacket, barely glancing at the rich furnishings and heavy brocade drapes. This had never been her home. She had felt more of a sense of belonging at Gregg's ranch— She shook her head. This was not the time to go there.

She found a thermostat and turned up the heat, then went to the kitchen. She had left packets of hot chocolate on her previous visit and began heating water. As she waited for it to boil she pulled out a telephone directory and jotted down a number. She needed advice and Clayton Ellridge was the only person she had who remotely resembled family.

She reached a receptionist and set up an appointment for the next morning. He was an investment counselor. She would pay him for his time.

Karen carried her mug into the den and turned on the gas log fire. The real thing would have been nice. Again she shook her head. She curled up in a large stuffed chair and pulled out the letter the lawyer had given her.

She studied it carefully, noted the yellowed envelope. Then taking a deep breath she lifted the flap and drew out the sheet of paper inside.

My darling daughter. If you are reading this, then that means I have departed this world within the last thirty years and this is the only thing of myself I can leave you.

Your name is Karen and you were six months old yesterday. I don't know if you are indeed the most beautiful baby ever born, but I do know you are the most beautiful one I've ever seen. I can't begin to imagine how beautiful you will be when you receive this letter. As a prejudiced father I already see great promise of that beauty.

Along with great beauty, you have it in your genes to possess great intelligence. As well as physical beauty, I hope you possess inner beauty as well, and that your intelligence will be guided by compassion and honesty.

I have withheld great wealth from you until this point in order to assure that you have found yourself in this world. I hope that you will have pursued goals and interests to the point of personal success and additional money will not change who you are, but perhaps enable you to fulfill a few dreams, yours or those of others you love.

As a McGraw, it seems to be our fate, be it blessing or curse, to love once and forever. By now, I hope you will have found that once-in-a-lifetime-love. It is my fondest hope that I will be the one who walks you down the aisle and hands you over to that special man who will stand beside you and tuck you inside his heart forever. If that has not yet happened, my daughter, let it happen. I wish for you the absolute happiness I have found in my life.

I have complete confidence in Phillip Vaughn. He understands my wishes concerning your future and will do everything possible to protect them. Let him know of any concerns and he will make everything right.

Your loving father, Jason McGraw.

Karen swiped helplessly at the tears flowing down her cheeks. *"Oh, Father, I miss you!"*

Gregg sat with feet propped on his desk, hands clasped behind his head, and stared at the door. *What was he doing here?* He had accomplished exactly nothing all week. With Karen gone, his life had ground to a halt.

What had Lori told him? To decide what, besides Karen, would make him happy for the rest of his life. And in saying that, she implied that when Karen came back she wouldn't want to leave again.

You have to let someone get close enough to care, Gregg.

That had been Lori's advice three years ago. He hadn't consciously followed it, but look where it had gotten him, anyway. As soon as he let Karen into his heart, she had left. Like all the others, he reminded himself bitterly.

He frowned. *Not like the others at all.* He had never really let them into his heart. When they failed to stand by him, his pride had been wounded, but never his heart.

On the other hand, Karen had stuck with him through the entire nightmare as they worked to identify Bobby and Juliana. She had effortlessly bewitched both Kelly and Kyle who loved her as much as he did. His grandmother had loved her long before he knew of their relationship. His mother had opened her heart to Karen and would gladly and thankfully welcome her as a daughter.

Decide what, besides Karen, will make you happy for the rest of your life.

Gregg swung his feet to the floor and sat up. He realized what Lori had been trying to tell him. A smile lifted the corners of his mouth.

Thanks, friend. Thank you, God.

Karen looked around the crowded attic. *Where to begin?* Whatever she hoped to find couldn't be anything new. She recognized many of the boxes and trunks that filled the space. The overhead light provided scant illumination so she flicked on her flashlight and played the beam across the floor and into the corners. *There!* The ray of light moved back, settled on a wood and brass trunk pushed into a corner.

Karen crawled over and drew a finger through the layer of dust that covered the old trunk. Drawing a deep breath, she held it as she reached for the latch. Whatever she might find, she intended to unearth the secrets of her past.

She didn't have room to raise the lid in the crowded corner so she pulled and pushed at the trunk until she had moved it to the center of the room, beneath the overhead light. She sneezed from all the dust she had stirred up, sneezed again. After waiting a moment for the dust to settle, she raised the lid.

A layer of yellowed plastic protected the contents beneath and she carefully moved it aside. *What was she looking for? Would she even know when she found it?*

She picked up a manilla envelope and caught her breath at the notation she read. *For Karen.*

Her fingers trembled as she undid the clasp and removed several photographs. The first photo showed a young man and woman in their wedding finery. Peering closer in the dim light, Karen recognized her mother, a much younger, softer, and happier version than she had been privileged to know. Did that mean the man beside her was Jason McGraw?

Karen turned the picture over and read a neat inscription. *Jason and Beth on their wedding day.* She turned it back to study the man again.

The second photo of the young man in a naval uniform caught Karen's breath. She could now see many of her own features in him. The curve of her eyebrows and her mouth and smile had definitely been passed down through the McGraw line.

Karen simply stared at the third photo, feeling as if she had picked up a mirror. *Kayleen McGraw Gillis,* the inscription read. Karen frowned. She had met her grandmother once, but this could not possibly be her. Besides, her grandmother had been introduced to her as Mimi Helen. Not likely that her name was Kayleen.

Karen shuffled through the rest of the pictures, finding one of her grandmother and verifying the name. She came back to the mysterious photo that could have been her identical twin. Who was this woman and why had she never known about her? It seemed obvious she was a relative and a close one. How could she find out?

CHAPTER SIXTEEN

Anna Watson dumped the bag of groceries on the table and scooped up the ringing phone.

"Flying M. May I help you?"

Silence.

"Hello. This is Anna. May I—"

An expulsion of breath. "Anna. This is Karen. I—"

"Karen, love, where are you?" Anna dropped into a chair, the groceries forgotten.

A short laugh. "Actually, at this moment, I'm sitting in my mother's attic covered in dust. I found a photo I need to ask you about."

"Go ahead."

"Does the name Kayleen McGraw Gillis mean anything to you?"

Anna clutched the receiver tightly. "It did. We were best friends for over twenty years."

"Who is she?"

"Jason's sister, a year or so younger."

A pause. "What happened to her?"

Anna drew a deep breath. "No one knows."

"What do you mean, no one knows?" Karen sounded near hysterics.

Anna swallowed, wishing she could be there to hold Karen. "She disappeared before you were born. She and her husband were caught in an avalanche. They found his body but gave up finding her after weeks of searching. There was no way she could have still been alive, but Jason refused to give up. He never quit hoping and then we lost him a year and a half later."

"How, exactly, did he die?"

"His mother blamed in on a broken heart. He threw himself into his work to the exclusion of everything else and fell asleep driving home."

"I see."

Anna hesitated, waiting for Karen to say more. Then, "Karen, dear, are you all right?"

"What? Oh, sure. Thanks, Anna. I'm sorry to have bothered you."

"Karen, wait—"

The receiver clicked. Anna slowly replaced hers, blinking away tears.

"Are you sure this isn't you?" Private detective Rodney Nolan bent over the photograph of Kayleen McGraw Gillis and looked up to study Karen.

"There's a date on the back," Karen said.

He turned the photo over. Looked at Karen again. "I can fax this to several of my buddies in the business and see if anything turns up. You say it's been thirty years?"

"I have someone doing an age progression drawing. I'd like you to fax them together."

He nodded. "Sounds like you know this business."

"Just a similar one. Investigative reporting. Well, I *was* an investigative reporter. I'm trying to retire."

"Retire?" He laughed. "At your age?"

Karen's eyes narrowed as she studied him. "Do you remember my name, Mr. Nolan?"

He glanced at the form he had been filling out. "Karen McGraw."

"And that name doesn't mean anything to you?"

He frowned. "Years ago, about thirty, I guess, seems there was a family around named McGraw. Lots of money. Old money."

She nodded. "Well, all that *old money* is mine now—and Kayleen's if we can find her." She pulled out a cashier's check and handed it to him. "This should cover your initial expenses. Let me know if there are additional costs."

He glanced at the check and his eyes bulged. He seemed to be struggling for breath. Then he slumped back in his chair.

"Miss McGraw, I have to tell you this is a long shot. I can't offer guarantees. I don't feel right taking your money—"

"I only ask that you try." She stood. "You know how to reach me. I'll get that age progression to you this afternoon."

Karen pulled into the parking lot of a modern office complex and looked up at the fifteenth floor. She waited for the bitterness and hurt that always blotted out everything else when she thought of Clayton Ellridge. Even blotted out the love she had felt for him until one day he had left and taken her sisters with him. Strangely, it did not come. Finally, she squared her shoulders and pushed open the car door.

Clayton Ellridge waited for Karen just inside the reception area. She eyed him warily. She had noted his presence at her mother's funeral, but had avoided speaking to him. Why, she could not say. She had defended him to Gregg. Didn't those same arguments apply where she was concerned?

She held out her hand. "Good morning—" She came to a dead stop. *What did she call him now?* Daddy had worked until she was twelve-years-old and before he left. Since then, she had carefully referred to him as her step-father when she had to acknowledge his existence at all.

"Karen!" He took her hand and then pulled her close in an embrace. She felt him tremble and drew back. He blinked away tears.

"Daddy?" Her own eyes filled with tears as she moved back into his arms and felt them close around her.

He put an arm around her shoulders and led her into his office. As he closed the door Karen found herself staring at the array of photos on his desk. Prominent among them were photographs of her at twelve, and a later one after she had grown up. She swallowed.

"I didn't know—" She reached out to touch a photograph.

"Didn't know that I loved you?" He sighed. "I guess you never received my letters. I finally stopped writing when I never got a reply."

Karen turned to Clayton and she knew he could see all the misery mirrored in her eyes.

"Why?" she whispered. "Why would mother do that? Why couldn't she love me? Why did she drive you away?"

He gently pushed her into a chair and handed her a glass of water before speaking. He sat down behind his desk and clasped his hands, then looked up to meet her gaze.

"Elizabeth was very ill, Karen. I didn't understand until after I left and could look back objectively. I think it all started with losing your father. She slipped into a deep and severe depression and never sought help.

"I've done a lot of research on the subject. Her world consisted of shades of gray. She tried to find happiness through manipulating others. She loved us—or should I say, she granted us approval—as long as we stayed within those dreary walls. Stray outside and we suffered her wrath."

Karen straightened. "I've done some research on depression myself." She fell silent, then shrugged. "I guess I was too close to make the connection, but a lot of what you say fits."

"Is that why you're here, Karen? To talk about your mother?"

She shook her head.

"That's not why I came, but I appreciate the information. Maybe it will help me forgive her. I've been talking to my father's lawyer, Phillip Vaughn, and my mother's will is invalid. My father left everything to me when I turned thirty, so the fact that she left a clause that I had to give up journalism doesn't hold any water."

"Whoa! What is this? Give up journalism. *She wanted you to give up journalism?*" He sounded incredulous.

Her mouth twisted. "I can't pretend to know what was in her mind, other than she never approved of my profession."

"And she tried to manipulate you through her will?"

Karen nodded, swallowing hard. "Actually, I had decided to follow through, not to get the money for myself. I figured if I gave it all away, I could do whatever I wanted. Then I found out it's all mine anyway, but I still want to set up trusts for Rebecca and Mickey's kids. I need your help with that."

"You're sure about this?" he asked.

"Absolutely."

"How can you be so different—" he broke off.

She shrugged. "—than my mother? Well, you just told me she was ill all those years. Maybe she wasn't really accountable. Or, since I just found out I look very much like my aunt Kayleen, maybe I'm more like her."

Clayton's head jerked up. "Kayleen McGraw?" He rammed his fingers through dark hair tinged with silver. "We dated in high school until she met Kevin Gillis." He shook his head. "I remember when they disappeared. Such a horrible tragedy. Jason was never the same, and I think that's when your mother started to go down. When you were born, he started to rally, but I think Elizabeth might have resented that he loved you more than her."

Karen shook her head. "I'm just learning that part of my heritage. I never even knew about Kayleen until yesterday." She debated for a moment whether to tell him about her search and decided not to.

"You do look very much like her," Clayton mused. "She was a wonderful person and a world class skier. So was Kevin. I always wondered how they could have been caught like that."

Karen wet her lips. "I understand her body was never found."

"I never heard if it was. After thirty years, you'd think something would turn up."

The journalist in Karen overrode her caution. *"Unless there was nothing to turn up."*

Clayton stared at her.

"I mean, what if there was no body? What if she was a good enough skier to ride it out, but maybe was injured and lost her memory?"

Clayton's gaze slid from hers. "I've thought that for thirty years. But I never knew who to talk to or what to do about it."

Karen sat up straighter. "Well, now you do."

Gregg's office door burst open and he looked up from the file box he was packing.

"Hey, Jack?"

"Hey, yourself." Jack frowned at Gregg for a moment, then shook his head. "I wish I could tell you you're making a mistake, but we both know you aren't. Do you have time for one last brainstorming session?"

Gregg sank into his chair, grateful for a break. "What's up?" He leaned back and put his feet on the desk.

Jack handed across two sheets of paper. "These just came in over the fax. I thought you might be interested."

Jack looked at the first and his feet crashed to the floor. "But—this looks like Karen!"

"That's what I thought," Jack said. "But it's the other photo that really interests me."

Gregg glanced at the second photo, back to the first. "Age progression?"

Jack nodded. "I know that lady, Gregg. I met her last Christmas when I was on vacation."

"So who's looking for her?"

"A PI out of Kansas."

"Kansas? Who is this lady supposed to be?"

"Kayleen—" Jack paused for effect, "—McGraw Gillis."

"McGraw?"

"I know. I'm thinking the same thing you are. Back to this lady I met. She's a skiing instructor. I hired her for my niece. I mentioned that she reminded me of someone I knew, meaning Karen, and she said she didn't know whether she had any family anywhere. She was in an accident thirty years ago and lost her memory. The only thing she retained was a love of skiing and the outdoors. She is basically a ski bum, initially hoping someone from her past would recognize her, and remaining with it because of her love of the sport."

Gregg swallowed. "Did you know Karen was an Olympic skier ten years ago? Before she broke her leg."

Jack's eyes widened. "Should I call this PI back?"

Gregg pushed his phone across the desk. "Use my phone."

Gregg stared at Anna. "Karen called you about this? And you didn't see any need to inform me?"

"Take it easy, Gregg!" Jack put his hand on Gregg's arm.

Anna shot him a grateful look. "Thanks." She turned back to Gregg. "What could I tell you? That she called near hysteria and asked me what I knew about Kayleen. She said she was in the middle of her mother's attic and had found a photo she needed to ask me about. The first time she was here I told her I knew her parents. I guess she thought I might know something about the rest of the family, too. As it turned out, Kayleen and I were friends up until she disappeared."

"You told Karen this?"

"I told her what I knew about Kayleen. It must have been quite a shock for her to pick up a photo and feel like she was looking into a mirror. I could hear it in her voice. I wanted to be there to hold her."

"She obviously doesn't accept the death theory," Jack put in, turning to look out a window.

"A lot of us didn't," Anna turned away to begin making coffee. "Especially Jason, Karen's father. He never gave up hoping until the day he was killed. Kayleen was just too good a skier to get caught in an avalanche."

"But they found her husband's body?"

Anna nodded. "He had broken a leg. My guess is that they were both trying to ski out of the avalanche. Kayleen, being the stronger skier was probably ahead of Kevin and may never have known he went down. If she survived, she was probably badly injured, perhaps suffered trauma to the head."

Anna looked at Jack. "If your friend is Kayleen, part of the reason she never remembered could be emotional. Guilt that she left her husband behind. Her mind can't accept that, and blocked everything out."

"So she was supposed to die along side him," Jack said gruffly.

Anna looked at him again. "Kayleen was one special lady. And she and Kevin had a storybook romance. I'm not saying it makes sense, but I think I do understand the forces at work here."

Gregg leaned against a counter and folded his arms across his chest. "Jack and I are flying up to talk to his friend in the morning," he told Anna.

She turned to stare at him, wet her lips.

"Without Karen?"

"Without Karen," he said firmly. "I can't afford to get her hopes up."

Anna's eyes snapped. "As much as I want to see the two of you together, you must drive her crazy. When are you going to realize how strong she is? She doesn't need or want to be coddled." She stalked from the room.

"Words I seem to recall—" Jack began.

"Don't start on me!" Gregg turned on him. "We don't tell Karen until we have some firm evidence."

Anna came back carrying a photo album.

"It's possible these photos could trigger her memory if she is Kayleen." Anna looked at Jack rather than Gregg. "A couple of other things. Kayleen had a scar about a half inch long just below her bottom lip and above her chin. She wasn't always such a great skier. And the little finger on her left hand—"

Jack made a strangled sound. "Let me guess. Whatever happened to it, she wasn't able to bend it. When she grasped the ski poles it stuck straight out."

Anna stared at him, her lips parted.

"And I saw the scar, too. We spent some time together. Had a couple of dates." He raked a hand through his hair.

Anna closed the photo album. "If you decide to take this, the photos are labeled. Please excuse me!"

"Ms. McGraw, your application is impressive. I would say your chances are better than average for being approved to adopt a child." The lawyer frowned at the application.

"But?" Karen prompted, wetting her lips.

"Well, I know the courts look at more than just the intended parent. You have nothing to offer in the way of extended family. And with your career, I don't see much sense of stability in your life."

Karen sighed. "That's true enough. I've heard all this before. But it seems to me that she doesn't have anyone now. We've grown quite close. I have to give this the best shot I can. For both our sakes."

"Then that's what we'll do!" The somber face softened in a smile. "Give it our best shot."

Gregg came in from a turn around the lake in his boat to find Jack with a newspaper spread across the kitchen table.

"Anything interesting?" he asked idly.

"Maybe the article about the abortion clinic over at Mason's Point."

Gregg stopped cold.

"Karen's article?" he forced himself to ask.

Jack looked up. "She's listed as a contributing journalist, but it isn't her byline. At the end there is a short article on her resignation."

"Resignation?"

"You didn't know?" Jack asked. "She stopped by the station to tell me before she left for Kansas."

"And you saw no reason to tell me?"

"Why would I? I assumed she would have told you herself if she wanted you to know."

Gregg said nothing.

"I guess your gloating was more than she could take," Jack suggested.

"What's that supposed to mean?"

"You made her life hell as a journalist. I guess she thought you would consider it a personal victory that she finally decided to call it quits."

"Funny how hollow that victory feels right now," Gregg said.

Gregg went into the kitchen and saw that Jack had left the paper for him. He picked it up and found it open to the abortion clinic article. He poured a glass of milk, carried it into the den, and settled back with the paper.

In the first paragraph, he learned that Karen had given a hot tip to a *Clarion* reporter and a couple of detectives. He calculated the time frame covered. She must have done that before the skiing trip! Why didn't she tell him? She knew how opposed he had been to her continuing with the story. She could have made everything right.

And why does she have to be the one to make everything right? a little voice prodded him. *There's no give and take in this relationship. Just your opinion and the wrong opinion.*

He threw the paper aside. How could she resign? She was the best.

And did you ever tell her that? Did she know how you felt about her work?

She tended to get too involved. I wanted to protect her from herself.

Like she wanted or needed that protection! All she ever wanted was your approval.

He sighed. I guess I messed things up good.

So what are you going to do about it?

I don't know. A lot depends on Kayleen.

CHAPTER SEVENTEEN

Gregg and Jack stood at the bar, trying to look like ski bums. Neither had any idea how to approach Jack's friend, whom he only remembered as Chrissy. They had brainstormed the situation during the entire flight and most of the drive to the lodge.

"What can I get for you gentlemen?" Then, as they turned, "Jack! Why didn't you tell me you were coming?"

Gregg found himself staring at a woman who looked so much like Karen that the hair on the back of his neck stood up. But instead of the ski clothing he expected, she wore a silk sweater over a matching broomstick skirt.

"Chrissy!" Jack found his voice. "What's this? I expected to find you on the slopes."

She bent and lifted the skirt slightly to reveal a walking cast on her left foot. "I made a bad landing the other day. They let me work in here so I won't be bored to death."

"So when do you get a break?" Jack asked.

She glanced at her watch. "Half hour."

"Would you be able to join us for lunch?" Jack asked.

"I don't know." Chrissy frowned. "Who's we? I haven't met your friend." She finally acknowledged Gregg's presence.

"Pardon me," Jack said with a laugh. "Chrissy, this is Gregg Watson. Gregg, meet Chrissy. Gregg and I work together."

"Work together?" Brown eyes identical to Karen's studied Gregg. *Much older and wiser brown eyes.* "And play together, too, it seems."

"Not exactly," Jack said. "This is more of a working vacation. I'll fill you in at lunch."

She nodded. "Now, back to my original question. What can I get for you gentlemen?"

"Coffee," Jack said. He glanced at Gregg. "Make that two coffees. I'll take cream. He'll have his black. Better yet, if you have some left over from yesterday, that'll work fine."

"Bad night?" Chrissy asked as she filled the cups.

"Bad week," Jack replied.

Chrissy threw him a glance and looked back at Gregg. "Does you friend talk, Jack?" Her voice was amused.

"Normally. Actually, this is the first time I've seen him struck dumb at sight of a beautiful woman." Jack picked up his coffee. "We'll be at this table in the corner."

"So," Jack asked when they were seated, "What do you think?"

Gregg glanced back at Chrissy. "Are you sure she's old enough to be Kayleen?"

Jack shrugged. "She doesn't know her exact age, but this life began in her early to mid-twenties and she's been Chrissy for thirty years. Kayleen disappeared when she was twenty-seven and has been gone for thirty years." He stirred his coffee, glanced at Gregg. "Your mother is about the same age."

Gregg frowned. "So."

"She doesn't look to be in her late fifties any more than Kayleen does."

"What does that mean? She looks like my mother."

"Come on Gregg. Anna is a beautiful woman and not old in any sense. Why didn't she remarry? Couldn't be lack of opportunity."

Gregg's frown deepened. "I never thought about it. I guess the same reason I haven't married. Who wants a man raising a ready made family? Who wants a woman raising her second family?"

Jack leaned back. "The twins are grown, so you can't use that as an excuse any longer. But for the sake of argument, I'll answer both questions. Karen has a heart big enough to love the whole world and she already loves your family. They all love her, too. The only hold out in the picture seems to be you."

"Jack—" Gregg's voice held a note of warning.

"And who wants a woman raising a second family? Maybe a man who never got around to having a family of his own."

Gregg stared at him. "Are we talking about someone I know here? Maybe someone I work with?"

Jack shot him a look. "Worked with, pard. Do you have a problem with that?"

Gregg leaned back and a smile began playing around his mouth. "Just one question."

"Shoot."

"Can I still call you Jack? Dad will be real hard to get used to."

Jack choked on his coffee.

"Why you—"

Chrissy put a couple of menus in front of them. "Why don't I take your lunch order, and by the time it's ready, I'll be able to join you." She glanced from one to the other. "Or is this a bad time?"

"Not at all." Gregg opened his menu. "Perfect timing."

She looked startled. "You can talk."

He grinned. "If I didn't say so earlier, nice to meet you, Chrissy."

"Same here. I'll be back in a couple of minutes."

Gregg looked at Jack. "I'm confused. I thought you had something going with Chrissy."

"Not as confused as I am. I was certain you had something going with Karen."

Gregg's face closed. "I'm not the one who left, Jack."

"So be the one who goes after her and brings her back. What better way to show her how you feel?"

Gregg studied the older man. "Have you always been such a romantic? Or is this a new facet to your personality?"

Jack shook his head and sipped his coffee. "I love Karen like the daughter I never had." He shrugged. "And I used to have high hopes for you, too. If God chooses to use me to keep you from making the same mistake I did, then I say, 'praise the Lord!'."

"What mistake?" Gregg sat up straighter.

"Why do you think I'm a fifty-eight year old bachelor with nothing but nieces and nephews to dote on?"

"I never thought about it. You are such an incorrigible flirt, I thought you wanted it that way."

Jack snorted. "The tears of a clown. Does anyone want it that way?"

Gregg considered Jack for a moment.

"How do you feel about opera?" he asked with seeming irrelevance.

"Opera?" Jack's head jerked up.

"And I'll have to teach you to ride a horse. No way will I have my mother involved with a greenhorn."

"Karen, I think it's time you went back home."

Her head jerked up to study the man behind the desk. The blood drained from her face and she wet her lips uncertainly.

"I thought—you wanted me to stay here."

Clayton Ellridge toyed with a letter opener. "Karen, there's nothing I'd like more than to have you stay here, if I thought that made you happy. But in the two weeks you've been here, I've watched you sink deeper and deeper into depression. Don't forget, I recognize the symptoms now." He studied her for a moment. "There's someone back in Colorado, isn't there?"

Karen sighed. "I don't know."

Clayton waited.

"When I left, I didn't exactly say I'd be back. I don't know if he even wants me anymore."

"Does he have a name?" Clayton asked gently.

"Gregg."

"Gregg Watson, perhaps?" Clayton probed further.

Karen looked up. "How would you know that?"

"Maybe he called this morning."

"Called? Called you?"

"Does he know how to reach you?"

"But he doesn't know who you are?"

"His mother does."

"I didn't tell him I would contact you."

"He took a chance."

She drew a deep breath. "So what did he call about?"

"He's flying up. Will be here at one-thirty to fly us back to his ranch."

"Us?" Karen whispered. "Why us?"

"Anna remembered that I used to know Kayleen. It seems that Gregg and his partner have found her. There doesn't appear to be any doubt. She has some identifying scars and injuries. Anna has spent a couple of days with her, but there has been no breakthrough in her memory. And no offense to you, my dear, but she never knew you existed."

Karen stared at him. "They found her. Why didn't you tell me?"

"I just found out this morning."

"How long has Gregg known?"

"I'm afraid you'll have to ask him."

"Where has she been all this time? Was she injured like we thought? And she has no memory—"

"Sounds like you and Gregg will have a lot to talk about on the flight back." He glanced at his watch. "You just have time to run home and pack a bag. I'll pick you up on the way to the airport a little after one."

Karen still sat, stunned. "They actually found her," she marveled. "This was the biggest gamble I ever took. The longest shot I ever played."

"I know." Clayton's eyes bored into her. "And if you give up your career in investigative journalism after this, it will be an unparalleled crime."

Her face fell. "Yeah? Well, I doubt that Gregg will agree with you."

Clayton frowned. "Why do you say that?"

"He doesn't think much of my career."

"Is that why you left?"

She shrugged. "I left because of mother's will. And because I needed to find some evidence of my own self-worth."

"Your own self-worth?" he echoed. "How could you doubt your worth?"

"How could I not?" She sniffed and swiped the back of her hand under her nose. "You left and my mother never wanted me. Then I fall in love with a man who thinks my career is all fluff and no substance."

Clayton stared at her. "We must be talking about a different Gregg Watson. I talked with him for several minutes this morning and that's not the impression I got at all."

"No?" Karen swallowed, trying not to remember too much. "Well, take it from me, he can be all charm when it serves his purpose."

"And what might be his purpose in charming me?"

Karen stared at him, wet her lips uncertainly.

Clayton looked smug. "Not that it hurts to have the father of the woman you love on your side, now that I think about it." He put the letter opener aside. "Go home, Karen. Pack that bag. I'll see you in an hour."

Gregg looked wonderful, Karen noted, as she studied him through her lashes. He greeted her step-father with easy charm and she watched as the two men summed each other up. His eyes flickered to her once, then he carefully avoided looking at her.

Her heart sank. Although she had no idea what to say to him, she had hoped for some sign, some indication as to how to proceed.

Dear God, please help me know what to do. I know I don't deserve him, but I love him beyond reason. I love his family. And I know he needs someone. I want to be that someone.

"Karen," the slightly impatient voice jolted her out of her musings and she looked up to see that Gregg had helped Clayton into the back seat and was holding the door for her to climb into the front seat.

She swallowed as she handed him her bag and watched him store it in the baggage area. His eyes burned into hers for a brief instant, so dark and intense she could not see the dark blue of his irises.

"What have you been doing with yourself?" he growled. "You look terrible."

Karen stared at him. Would it matter how she looked if he didn't care?

Some imp inside her took over. She raised herself on tiptoe and pressed her mouth to his as her arms curled around his neck. She felt him stiffen and his hands tightened at her waist.

She pulled back. "You don't." She gave him her most radiant smile. "I've never seen you look better. Obviously, you haven't missed me." She turned away from him and climbed into the plane and reached for the seat belt.

Then suddenly she was standing on the tarmac and Gregg's hands gripped her arms.

"Yeah, well, I've been a little busy," he said. "As far as missing you, that's something we'll take up later. Until then, think about this!" His head bent and his mouth claimed hers.

All thoughts of protest died in a whimper as her arms again went to circle his neck, to draw his head closer to hers. She kissed him with all the love she could no longer hold back.

Gregg raised his head as a tremor shook him. He stared into her eyes.

Karen reached up to trace her finger tip around his mouth, her own softening into a smile. "By all means. Let's take this up later!"

Anna and Jack stood on either side of Kayleen as they watched Gregg, Karen and Clayton walk toward the house. They had not told her who would be returning with Gregg and watched for any sign of recognition.

"What a beautiful young woman!" Kayleen said softly. Her breath caught. "And who is that gorgeous man?"

Anna looked again. Obviously, Kayleen couldn't be referring to Gregg, and yes, she was right. Anna had forgotten how attractive Clayton Ellridge was. The best part had always been that he had no idea how attractive the opposite sex found him. Her lips curved into a smile. Before Kevin Gillis, Kayleen and Clayton had been close. Was it possible that some degree of attraction might have survived all the intervening years?

"The young lady is your niece, Karen McGraw, the one who initiated the search for you, and hopefully, soon to be my daughter. The good-looking man is her step-father, Clayton Ellridge."

Kayleen continued to stare at Clayton. "Did I know Clayton before?"

Anna stiffened. "Why do you ask?"

"Something familiar—" She broke off. "Silly thought. Of course he's just here with his daughter." She laughed. "It must be hard to let go of a daughter like that. She's perfect."

Anna looked at Kayleen curiously, but there was no trace of vanity in her voice or on her face. Did she not realize that in describing Karen she included herself?

"She is," Anna agreed. "She looks so much like you, it's uncanny."

Kayleen looked startled and turned again to study Karen. "Oh, no. I never looked like that."

Anna laughed. "Fortunately, you did. Otherwise Karen might never have asked enough questions to decide to launch a search for you. She couldn't believe she had a relative who looked so much like her and she didn't even know she existed."

The three mounted the back steps and Kayleen trembled slightly as she turned to meet them.

Karen stopped cold as she came face-to-face with her long lost aunt. The resemblance still rocked her, and Karen unconsciously put a hand to her own face. As in a trance, Kayleen followed through with the same gesture.

Clayton made a choking sound and drew a trembling breath.

"Kayleen, I never thought I'd see you again!" he said, his voice cracked with emotion. "You look wonderful!"

Kayleen shifted her gaze to his, stared transfixed. "I—so do you," she said huskily. "I feel as if I should know you."

"It's been a long time." He caught the hand she had extended and brought it to his lips. *"Bonjour, ma cherie."*

Kayleen drew in her breath softly. *"Bonjour, mon ami."*

Clayton lowered her hand, barely breathing. He took her hand in both of his. "You never did get that accent quite right, did you, Kayla?"

"Clay," she whispered. She reached up to touch his face. "It really is you." She closed her eyes. "I remember being heartbroken when you dumped me for—" she opened her eyes.

Clayton's eyes twinkled. "Keep going. Curly red hair. Legs to die for."

Kayleen gave a snort of disgust. "Peggy Lou Morton. She couldn't ski worth anything."

"She couldn't. Dumping you was the biggest mistake I ever made."

She tilted her head. "Why was that?"

"By the time I stopped being dazzled by red hair and emerald eyes, you had met Kevin."

"Kevin?" she whispered. Her lips trembled. She put a hand to her mouth. "Kevin!" The primal cry tore from her lips.

Clayton caught her in his arms as she swayed and Anna reached for a chair to lower her into. Both Clayton and Anna knelt beside her.

Karen felt a hand on her arm and looked up to see Gregg beside her. He motioned with his head that they should leave. She let him lead her outside.

Karen folded her arms on the rail surrounding the porch. "He told me they had dated at one time. I had no idea they had been that close."

Gregg stood beside her, leaning over to rest his arms on the same rail. "I want to know why you decided to search for her."

"Well, I found her photo, and Anna told me who she was and what had happened to her. I went to the library and searched the archives and pieced together as much of the story as was known. I didn't think there was enough evidence that she was dead."

"Except that she had been missing for thirty years."

"But her wallet and wedding rings were found in Kevin's back pack. She would have had no identification and no evidence that she belonged to anyone. If she suffered a concussion, she might have been unconscious for days or weeks. Whoever found her may not have heard the missing persons report. I simply couldn't believe that nothing had turned up in thirty years."

"So tell me that you aren't serious about giving up journalism," Gregg said, turning to look at her. "You can't, Karen. You're too good. You don't need your mother's money, not if it means giving up your work."

"Funny. Clayton said something similar this morning."

"Did you believe him?"

"I believe I said something to the effect that I doubted you would agree with him." Karen looked up to meet his eyes.

His gaze did not waver. "I had a lot of time to think and reconsider. I know I never supported you, not even about the abortion clinic. I was wrong. But all I wanted was for you to be safe, and you wouldn't let me protect you."

"The only thing I needed protection from was your tongue lashings—"

"Along with a dozen or so teenage thugs and one deranged nephew," he reminded.

"Yeah, well—" She looked away.

"Karen, I have enough money for both of us. Don't accept the terms of your mother's will—"

"That sounds like bribery. You already tried blackmail."

He made a growling sound of frustration. "And I'm about ready to try abduction if that's what it takes." He towered over her, wrapped a hand in her hair, pulled her head back. "How about it? Will it take dragging you off to my lair to get your attention?"

Karen swallowed. "You had my attention long before you knew I existed."

"I doubt that." His breath fanned across her lips. "Marry me, Karen."

"I can't marry you unless I give up my job."

He stared at her. "Why not?"

"You trained me well. Cops and reporters don't mix. I don't want to spend the rest of my life fighting with you."

"You won't have to."

"I won't? Why not?"

"Because," he said smugly, "I'm not a cop any more."

She pulled back from his embrace. "Say that again."

"I resigned. I'm a rancher now. Jack is going to be my foreman—as soon as he learns to ride. He's been hitting on my mom, so I need him around so I can keep an eye on him."

Karen stared at him.

"Say something." He brushed her lips softly with his.

"You quit your job?" she said.

"Yes."

"But I can't quit mine?"

He frowned. "Not unless there is something else you want to do a thousand times more."

"Actually, there is."

"And what might that be?"

"I'll get to that," she said. She glanced at the house. "I've been learning what it's like to be a daughter again, with the love of a parent. I hoped I might get to be a niece, too. Do you think I will get to meet my aunt anytime soon?"

"You know," he turned her back toward the door. "That might be just what the doctor ordered.

CHAPTER EIGHTEEN

Gregg pushed open the back door and held it for Karen. They found Jack in the kitchen making coffee. He looked up.

"Perfect timing." He put the tray in Karen's hands. "It's about time you put in an appearance. Kayleen needs a distraction and you're the best there is." He gave her a quick kiss on the cheek. "She doesn't bite. She's every bit as wonderful as you are."

Karen glanced at Gregg and he nodded, giving her a quick smile of encouragement. He blew her a kiss.

"Go on. I'll say a little prayer for you."

Karen hesitated a moment and then walked slowly out of the room.

Gregg released his breath. "She walked into that abortion clinic without hesitation. Now, she's scared to death to meet a close relative."

Jack looked at him, then reached over to pour another cup of coffee and hand it to Gregg.

"Her heart wasn't at risk at the abortion clinic. Now it is."

Gregg's head jerked up. "What do you mean?"

"It's terribly important to Karen that her aunt accept her. She hasn't had any close family for so long." He stared into his cup. "Wouldn't it be great if her step-father and her aunt could resume that relationship?"

"I was thinking the same thing," Gregg said. Then he punched Jack in the arm. "I never knew you were such a romantic!"

Jack shrugged. "When I care about people, I want them to be happy. You know how I feel about Karen."

Gregg sipped his coffee and made no reply.

"Speaking of which—" Jack began.

Gregg put down his cup. "Let's not go there. I'm taking the boat out. Wanna come along?"

Jack glanced toward the den, then back at Gregg. "Sure. Why not? Beats standing around here walking on egg shells."

From the balcony, Karen watched Gregg and Jack walking back from the lake. They appeared to be deep in conversation and neither looked up.

Her gaze rested on Gregg, memorizing every detail. Her thoughts went back to the kiss they had promised to get back to later and her lips curved into a smile. She loved him. And just maybe he still wanted her. She didn't intend to leave here without finding out.

"Where's Karen?" Gregg asked as he and Jack came through the back door. "And Kayleen?"

Anna looked up from the table where she and Clayton were sitting. "Resting. This has been very emotional for both of them." She looked back at Clayton. "Clay and I have been catching up on the past thirty years or so." She stood up. "I'll check with Marie about dinner."

Silence followed Anna's departure. Jack picked up the coffee pot.

"More coffee?" he asked Clayton, filling a cup for himself.

Clayton looked at his empty cup. "Why not? Who knows when I'll get coffee this good again?"

Jack filled his cup. "My thoughts exactly." He glanced at Gregg. "As bad as Gregg's coffee is, I won't even have that when I go back to the office."

Gregg quirked an eyebrow as he dropped into a chair across from Clayton. "I'm counting on that. You won't last long without my coffee."

Jack sat down and sipped his coffee for a moment.

"So," Clayton looked from one to the other. "I understand you two found Kayleen. How exactly did that come about?"

"Well, we were both struck by her resemblance to Karen when she was younger," Jack explained. "But when I saw the age progression drawing, I realized I had met her a few months ago—around Christmas. And she had dropped a hint or two then that she had no memory prior to thirty years ago."

Clayton shook his head. "It's absolutely amazing how these things work out. There's no denying the hand of God at work in a case like this."

Gregg cleared his throat. "It seems to me that you played a rather major part yourself. We hadn't been able to prod any memory until you started speaking French to her."

Clayton smiled. "We met in French class in high school. She could do a lot of things well, and some things superbly, but speaking French wasn't one of them. Kissing her hand and speaking French to each other became a joke. I don't know what made me think of it. Just seeing her again, I guess."

"I gather this lady is more than a little special to you," Jack guessed.

Clayton shook his head and sighed. "I have no idea how to answer that. It's been thirty years. Most of the time I believed she was dead. And she hasn't even known I existed. I don't know what happens next. She's extremely vulnerable right now. So is Karen." He cradled his cup in his hands. "I've been thinking the best thing I can do for both of them right now is back off, give them breathing room, and go back to Kansas."

"Bad idea," Jack said.

"Really bad idea," from Gregg.

"You would leave me again?" The choked question snapped three heads around to stare at Karen.

She had changed into jeans and a T-shirt and her hair hung loose around a face scrubbed free of make-up. She looked all of twelve years old and Gregg felt his heart twist with pain for her.

Clayton must have been thinking along the same lines. "You look the way you did when you were twelve," he said gruffly.

"I still need you as much as I did when I was twelve," she replied.

"Sweetheart," Clayton crossed the room to take her in his arms. "I'm not leaving you permanently. I just thought you and Kayleen need some time alone. To get to know one another."

She shook her head. "Right now she has too much pain to know I even exist. If you go back, take me with you."

"And leave me here alone after I finally discover that I have the two of you? That would be too cruel, don't you think?"

Gregg looked up to see Kayleen standing behind Clayton and Karen.

"You're right," Clayton said. "Bad idea. *Really bad idea.*" He reached out to draw Kayleen into the circle of his embrace. "When we leave, we will go together."

Jack stood up and hauled Gregg to his feet. "Come along, Pard. You were going to show me how to muck out stalls—"

Anna laughed. "No one is going anywhere for a few hours. Dinner in ten minutes if anyone needs to wash up."

Gregg strode from the room, glancing at Karen as he did. Had he brought her home only to lose her to her newly found family? He had to give her this time. He couldn't be selfish. *But how he wished those were his arms offering her comfort!*

"Karen went down to play with the kittens," Anna informed Gregg as he walked into the kitchen. She glanced at him and did a double take.

"My, my. Looks like we've been doing a wee bit of thinking, now haven't we?"

Gregg smiled at her imitation of his grandfather's brogue. "You know me too well."

"If it helps any, Karen doesn't look much better. For the first time in her life she has people who love her and they are pulling her in opposite directions." She handed Gregg a cup of coffee.

"I know she has to go back with Kayleen," Gregg said. "I'm just afraid she will stay. I don't think I have enough to offer her."

214

"You've asked her to stay?" Anna asked.

"Does asking her to marry me count?"

Anna stared at him, her eyes growing misty. "Oh, Gregg!"

Gregg went over to look out the window. "I didn't get a yes, but at least it wasn't a resounding 'no' this time."

"This time?"

He nodded briefly. "I asked her to marry me during the skiing trip."

"And got a resounding 'no'?"

"Not exactly?"

"Well, what did you get?"

He frowned at her in mock indignation. "Does being my mother—"

"Yes, it does."

He sighed. "What can I say? She left."

Anna gave an impatient sigh. "Before that."

"I think she felt she had to find herself. Her note said that until she did, she wasn't any good for either of us. She wasn't what I needed."

Anna swallowed. "Give her time, Gregg. I know she loves you."

He shrugged in defeat. "To date, I don't think she knows what love is. It certainly isn't anything you can depend on, that you would want to stake a future on."

Anna touched his face. "I'm praying that that will all change for her. That the love she sees here will convince her."

Gregg nodded. "Yeah. So am I." He drained his cup. "And just to stack the deck a little more in my favor, I still have a few cards up my sleeve."

Gregg stood for a moment and watched Karen playing with the kittens. In cut-off jeans, an eyelet blouse and her hair loose, she still looked more like the twelve year old he had seen last night. She had kicked off her sandals and sat curled in the loose hay, teasing a kitten with a straw. Another kitten pounced on a bare toe and she drew it back with a giggle.

"Could I interest you in a kitten, little girl?" Gregg drawled. "They come from the very best McClaren bloodlines. Pure barn cat."

After a momentary start, Karen looked up at him. "I always thought I was allergic to cats, but I haven't sneezed once."

"That's a good sign." He met her gaze. "Does that mean you never had a kitten?"

"I never had any kind of pet. Except once a mouse that lived in the basement. I fed it cheese." She got to her feet. "Then my mother found it and set a trap with cheese. I wasn't much interested in pets after that."

"Karen—" Gregg broke off, knowing any words he might say would be inadequate. Then an idea hit him.

"Around here, it's better not to become too attached to the mice, either. That's why we have the cats. They are known throughout the county as great mousers. Zelda has already brought in a mouse for a training session with these kittens."

She looked up, eyes wide. "How—does she do that?"

He shrugged. "She brings in a live mouse, lets the kittens play with it for a while, then dispatches it. They aren't old enough to eat mice, yet, but she shows them that's what it's all about. You can consider that cruel, or simply the law of survival. I don't see it as being any different than a man who raises cattle for food."

216

Karen nodded. "I could never get too caught up in a lot of the animal right's issues. Don't worry." She gave a weak smile. "I still like your cats. *Bloody murderers though they may be!*"

At that moment, Zelda jumped up on the door of the stall for Gregg to scratch behind her ears. Her purr filled the small space.

Gregg stroked her. "Did you hear what she called you?" he murmured to the dainty gray cat. "Bloody murderer, indeed! See what happens when you get involved with a bleeding heart."

Karen watched him, her gaze softening, her lips curving into a smile.

"If we're going to stoop to name calling here," she said, "then I declare you a world-class fraud, Officer Watson."

"Fraud?" He still spoke to the cat. "What do you suppose she is raving about now, Zel?"

"Zelda, do you know that your friend here, the big softie who is petting you and whispering sweet nothings to you, tries to pass himself off as a tough, macho, cave-bear type. In fact, Zelda, that is the only side of him he wants me to see. What do you suppose that says about him?"

He picked up the cat and cradled her beneath his chin. She rubbed the top of her head along his jaw line, her purr increasing to a crescendo.

"What say you to that, Zellie?" He rubbed his chin against her head and her eyes closed in ecstasy. "We know where we stand with each other, don't we? We have no need of deception or pretense or foolish games." He placed her gently inside the stall. "Now, I think your babies want breakfast. That's a good girl."

Zelda immediately plopped down to be pounced upon by four squirming, meowing balls of fur. As they settled down to nurse, she began grooming all within reach, her contented purr again filling the stall.

Karen watched the gentle scene, touched by the rightness of it all. Jealous that on some level, Zelda could relate to Gregg in a way she never had. Would she ever know where she stood with him? *Or he with her?*

She froze, slowly raising her eyes to his. *That was their problem in a nutshell!* Neither could give everything. Neither could trust completely. Both held too much back as protection against betrayal. What had he said to Zelda?

We have no need of deception or pretense or foolish games.

Dear Father, help me to trust Gregg. He has asked me to marry him. What more do I need from him? He has risked everything and still I hold back.

"I told Clayton we would leave at ten. I'll fly the three of you back to Kansas." Gregg's voice was void of emotion.

Karen wet her lips, still staring at him. "So soon?"

He shrugged. "The consensus seems to be that the sooner Kayleen is back in the house where she grew up, the better it will be for her. She needs to be surrounded by familiar things."

"That doesn't include me," Karen said before she could think.

Gregg swallowed. "You are the most important thing in her world. The only link to the brother she loved. Clayton was a good friend. Maybe he will be again. But at the moment you are the only fixed point in her universe."

"You—want me to go!" She shook her head in disbelief. "I thought you would at least try and talk me out of—"

"I won't do that to you," Gregg said, holding her gaze. "I can't put that kind of pressure on you. We both know you have to go. Only you can decide how long you have to stay."

"This isn't fair!" Karen said. "A few weeks ago, I didn't have anyone—"

The stall door still between them, Gregg reached out to put a hand behind her neck, to draw her face to his.

"Be careful what you wish, my love!" His lips touched hers in the briefest of kisses, then he was gone.

CHAPTER NINETEEN

Father, help me! I can't do this. Karen tore her gaze from Gregg as he unloaded baggage and helped Clayton load it into the car. *I can't let him leave without me, and I have to stay here for Kayleen. Please—*

"Gregg, is there any way you could be available for a few more days?" Kayleen asked, her voice uncertain.

He straightened to look at her. "What did you have in mind?"

"Well, Clay and I have been talking, and I need to get my things from Utah. If I could hire you to fly me there—apparently I can afford that now—then I could pack everything and ship it here. I'll probably sell my car. It's hardly worth trying to drive back. If you have time, then you could fly me home, or I could probably find—"

"I only see one problem," Gregg said.

"What would that be?"

"What's this about hiring? Consider it a favor."

"But you've already done far too much," Kayleen protested.

"According to whom? No one can do enough to make up for what you've lost. Thirty years. The years when you might have had a daughter like Karen. When you might have had grandchildren. I would consider it an honor to do whatever it takes to help you get your life back in order."

Kayleen swallowed, blinked. Brushed at the tears coursing down her face. She reached up to kiss Gregg's cheek.

"And I've been told," she said, loud enough for Karen to hear, "that my niece is having trouble making up her mind about marrying you. Funny. My first impression is that she's a lot smarter than that."

Gregg gave her a conspiratorial grin. "As you say. Funny. But they do say looks can be deceiving." Over her head, he saw Karen make a face and stick her tongue out at him.

"I'll have to have a long talk with her," Kayleen said.

"You do that." Gregg caught her hands. "And I'll consider it payment in full."

"My pleasure."

Karen turned away. Closed her eyes. *Thank you, dear Father. I won't blow it this time.*

"But of course you will spend the night here," Kayleen said to Gregg. "There are dozens of rooms. Surely at least one is habitable." She turned to Karen as she entered. "Isn't there?"

Karen looked startled. "I beg your pardon?"

221

"How are you fixed for spare bedrooms? For Gregg?"

"And for you. I had no time to get anything ready. You will probably want Mother's suite. All we have to do is pull the dust covers off."

"And where have you been sleeping?" Kayleen asked.

Karen shrugged. "My room. But then I guess you wouldn't know anything about that."

Kayleen grinned. "Wanna bet? Could it be the one under the eaves with window seats?"

Karen's mouth fell open, but she recovered quickly, her eyes sparkling with mischief.

"It's mine! I saw it first."

"Not really, but—"

"Children! Children." Gregg stepped between them with mock seriousness. "I'm sure we can find suitable rooms for all."

Kayleen laughed. "I'm sure Beth's rooms will be fine. Is there still a room off the den? Maybe we can put Gregg there."

"I've been—sort of using it," Karen said reluctantly. In the silence that followed she looked up to see both Gregg and Kayleen staring at her.

"How does one 'sort of' use a room?" Kayleen asked.

"Well—I've been using the den as an office, and—I turned that room into a dark room."

"A dark room?" It was Gregg who spoke.

Karen sighed. "I didn't intend to tell you this way. Remember when you said I could only quit my job if there was something I wanted to do a thousand times more?"

"And you said that actually there was."

She nodded. "Well, I decided that rather than continue to, as you so rightly put it, *expose the seedy underbelly of polite society*, I wanted to try and capture everything that was right and good and beautiful in the ordinary world."

"You're a photographer?" Kayleen guessed.

Karen shrugged. "I've always taken pictures. Mostly to accompany my articles. But many times, just because something interested me or caught my eye. I thought it was time to find out if I have anything worth while."

"And?"

"Who knows? I just got started a few days ago. We can give Gregg my room and I can sleep—"

"Oh, no you don't," Kayleen said. "I know something about photography. Lead the way, my dear. I have to see this."

Gregg stood in the middle of the room, shocked and humbled. Many of the images Karen had captured were familiar to him. Amanda and Michael, Rosa and Angela, and other faces from the children's home and the nursing home. Kelly and Kyle. Jack. The two white crosses. And countless other scenes and faces that meant nothing to him. *Or they shouldn't have.* But somehow, all the images spoke to him. Reached out and touched him.

Kayleen shivered. "This is uncanny! I've never seen any of these faces, except Jack, but I feel I know them all. That I should know them all. That I want to know them all." She looked at Gregg. "Am I making sense?"

"Perfect sense," he assured her.

"Did you know about this?"

"What do you think?" He sat down on the edge of a table. "I may love your niece to distraction, but there are depths to her I never suspected." He glanced around the room. "This is one of them." He looked back at Kayleen. "Am I right? Are these as good as I think they are?"

"In my opinion, yes. But I have a friend who publishes this sort of work. I can arrange for Karen to talk to her while we're in Utah."

Karen had disappeared, presumably to get their rooms ready for the night. Gregg frowned, looked at Kayleen.

"Go ahead. But don't be surprised if she doesn't welcome your help."

"What do you mean?"

"I have a feeling this is something she wants to do on her own."

"From what I've heard, she's had to do everything on her own her whole life. Don't worry. I'll make this a bonding experience for us."

Gregg studied her for a moment, grinned. Kayleen was every bit as strong willed as Karen. If anyone could change Karen for her own good, it would be Kayleen.

"Can I ask a favor?" he said now.

Kayleen pulled her gaze away from a photograph. "Sure. Anything."

"If Karen decides not to marry me, can I still keep you?"

Midnight had long passed and Gregg watched Karen from the door of the darkroom. Sensing his presence, she glanced up and caught her breath.

"What are you doing still awake?" she whispered.

"I could ask you the same question. Why are we whispering?"

"So we don't wake Kayleen." She glared at him. "I'm not the one who has to be up to flying a plane at—"

224

"O-dark-thirty." He moved into the room and reached for a photo.

She took the picture from him. "O-what?"

He shrugged. "Pilot lingo. O-dark-thirty. Before dawn." He looked around. "What are you doing?"

"Kayleen suggested I put together a portfolio so that she could show a publisher she knows. I thought if I humored her, it might make her feel that she belongs. Give her a sense of being needed—you know, helping me."

Gregg smothered a grin. "Yeah, I know. Nice of you to think of her feelings. Who knows, she might even be able to help. Try to show a little enthusiasm, will you?"

Karen studied him through her lashes. "You like her, don't you?"

He sat on the edge of a table, arms folded across his chest. "What's not to like?"

"Nothing. She's wonderful."

"So what's your problem?"

"No problem." Karen bent her head. "The two of you seem to have developed quiet a friendship very quickly."

"That can happen when two people discover a common interest. Besides, I find her extremely likeable."

"Not like me, huh?"

Gregg studied the part of her face he could see. Then he reached over and caught her arm, pulling her to stand in front of him. He removed the folder from her and tucked her hands inside his.

"I wouldn't say that. You have your moments."

Her eyes jerked to his and she tried to free her hands.

"Moments aren't enough—"

"They're enough for a start!" He straightened to pull her close. "Wasn't there something we were supposed to get back to?"

She leaned back in the circle of his arms, toyed with his lapels, a smile playing around her mouth. "I can't think of anything."

"My mistake." His arms fell.

She sucked in her breath. "Don't you dare!" She threw her arms around his neck and pulled his head down to hers. "I thought it would only be a few hours. But you've made me wait two days! And if it wasn't for Kayleen, you would be gone by now."

"As I said, she's extremely likeable."

"I don't want to talk about her!"

"No? But you just—"

"Will you kiss me?" Her voice grew husky. "Please, Gregg!"

"Well, when you ask like that—"

"Don't talk!"

"As you wish—"

With a groan she reached up to press her mouth to his.

As if released, he speared his hands into her hair and took over the kiss, then raised his head to cradle her against his chest.

"Ummmm," she murmured. "Wonderful!"

He pressed his lips to her forehead. "I strive to please."

"No," she pulled back. "You always excel. You don't even have to try." She reached up to touch his face. "Gregg—"

"Yes, love?"

She sighed, buried her face against his shoulder. "I want to marry you."

He went still. "That isn't a yes."

Another sigh. "Not yet. But close. Very, very close."

"*Hardly worth trying to drive back!* What was the woman thinking?"

Karen looked up from her scrutiny of the tiny garage under Kayleen's cabin to see Gregg bent over an old car. She walked over to it.

"Whatever it was, I'd have to agree with her," Karen said. She wiped off a smudge of dirt. Bent for a closer look. "On second thought—" Her eyes flew to Gregg's. "Isn't this—"

"Go on," he prompted.

"Isn't this a classic Mustang? I'm not sure of the year . . . '63 . . . '65 . . . maybe. I covered a convention once."

Gregg popped the hood. "'65." He gave a low whistle. "Engine looks almost mint."

"It only has about 20,000 miles," Kayleen said from the doorway. "I never drove it much. To town for groceries every couple of weeks. I didn't have any place to go that I knew of."

Gregg closed the hood. "Do you know what this car is worth?"

She shrugged. "It's over forty years old. What can it be worth?"

Gregg shook his head. "To you, obviously not much." He grinned. "I'll give you $12,000."

Kayleen stared at him. "Gregg, I'm telling you, it isn't worth $1200. I thought I'd just give it to a friend—"

"$15,000. I have to have this car.""

"Then take it. Since I'm giving it away, anyway. Consider it fair exchange for flying me up here—"

"No, Kayleen, you don't understand. This is a valuable car. It is considered a collector's car. People pay outrageous prices for them. I happen to know Jack would sell his soul for this car."

"Jack? What does Jack have to do with this?"

"He'd love this car. I want to give it to him as a wedding gift when he marries my mother."

Kayleen started laughing. "This is too funny!"

Gregg and Karen both stared at her, waiting for her to explain. At last she caught her breath and wiped her eyes.

"I gave Jack a ride in this car last winter. He fell in love with it. Since he played a rather major role in finding me, I thought I'd let him have it! So," she smothered a giggle, "can we stop haggling over the price?"

Gregg held out his hand and Kayleen clasped it. "Done."

Karen cleared her throat. "Um—uh, just how do you plan to get it back to Colorado?"

Kayleen looked at Gregg. "Well, I figured when I told Jack it was his, he'd find a way to get it home. But I gather you had something else in mind?"

"Actually I do. I'll drive it into Salt Lake tomorrow and get someone started on the restoration. That will probably take a few weeks. Then I'll have Kyle fly me up to drive it back." He turned to Kayleen. "Do you think you can wrap things up here and be ready to leave by noon tomorrow?"

"Sure. Maybe sooner than that. I hate to impose—"

"It isn't that." Gregg ran a hand through his hair. "I've been keeping an eye on the weather. Right now, we're between two fronts. I don't want to leave too soon, or we'll overtake the one between us and home. On the other hand, if we don't get out by noon tomorrow, we'll be racing the one that is coming in behind us."

"Enough said. I'll be ready whenever you say. I never had much. Never wanted much. Funny how all along I had everything if I had only known who I was. I wonder if somehow, subconsciously, I did know."

"They have made great strides in understanding the sub-conscious mind in the past thirty years," Karen said gently. "If you need to talk to someone, I have done research on the subject. I could introduce you to some of my contacts."

Kayleen nodded. "Maybe. But right now, I think the best thing for me is going to be renewing my relationship with Anna and Clay and anyone else who might be around who would remember me."

"If it's all right with you, we'll spend tomorrow night at the ranch before flying on to Kansas. That'll give you some more time with my mother."

Kayleen nodded. "I was hoping for a chance to talk with her again soon. I've remembered a couple of things I want to ask her."

CHAPTER TWENTY

"That's interesting," Gregg mused as he turned the plane downwind to line up with the landing strip at his ranch.

Both Karen and Kayleen glanced in the direction he was looking.

"What's interesting?" Kayleen asked.

"We have a visitor. I recognize the airplane. I'm just not sure who might be flying it." He turned final and began his descent.

"That little yellow Piper Cub? I once knew someone who flew one of those. My friend Jean gave up her modeling career to marry Hal Holland."

Gregg made a strangled sound. "Small world." The plane touched down and Gregg taxied toward the hangar where the other plane waited.

Kayleen glanced at him. "That can't be Hal's plane!"

"I'm afraid it is. And I'm also afraid his daughter, Kris, is the pilot. I can only think of one other person who might fly it this far, and the last I heard, he was still recuperating from a broken leg."

"Jean and Hal have a daughter," Kayleen mused. "How are they? I can't wait to hear—"

Gregg sighed. "I never knew Jean. She died when Kris was quite young. Hal passed away a few months ago. I've been worried about Kris. She's too much a loner."

"Sounds a lot like her father." Kayleen shook her head. "I wonder how many of my friends are no longer around. Finding out who I am may be even more painful that I'd counted on."

"Knowing who you are all along is no guarantee that there won't be pain," Gregg said flatly. The plane came to a stop and he cut the engine.

Kayleen turned to him. "Oh, Gregg, I'm sorry. I wasn't thinking. I know you have lost so much—"

Gregg reached over to cover her hand with his. "We all have," he said gruffly. "Look at all Karen has lost. And Kris, as well. Speaking of whom—" He nodded to draw Kayleen's attention.

Kayleen turned her head and sucked in her breath. "But I thought you said Jean—"

"That's not Jean. That is her daughter, Kristen. I have heard the only physical difference is that she has Hal's green eyes."

"What a combination! She must be just about perfect. We all thought Jean was crazy until we met Hal."

Karen had sat silently throughout this exchange. *Who was this Kris?* She wondered now, feeling the tentacles of jealously reaching out to ensnare her. She watched as Gregg pushed open the door and leaped to the ground to catch the slender blonde in his arms.

"Gregg!"

"Princess!"

"I'm sorry for dropping in without warning—"

"You know you're always welcome."

A husky laugh. "I wonder if you'll still think so in a couple of hours."

Gregg put her away from him. "What happens in a couple of hours?"

"For starters, I think I'm stuck here for awhile." She turned to frown at the growing cloud bank to the west.

"Good point. We need to secure your plane. If I move the tractor out, we can make room for it." He turned back to see Kayleen and Karen standing a few feet away. "This is Karen and Kayleen," he said easily. "Ladies, meet Kris. You can head for the house before the storm hits, or—" he dug keys from his pocket, "—if anyone knows how to drive a tractor—"

Kayleen grabbed for the keys. "Does a snow plow count? Where do you want it?"

"East side of the barn."

A gust of wind from the storm front almost lifted the small wood and fabric airplane off the ground. Kris grabbed one of the struts.

"Weren't you cutting things a little close?" Kris asked Gregg as he helped her push the plane into a corner of the hangar. "I know my father taught you better than that."

Gregg threw her a grin. "Yes, well, the best laid plans, and all that. It's been an interesting day." He stepped back to admire the classic little airplane.

232

"It still looks like new. A wonderful restoration."

"It was Dad's last project. I can't let it go."

Gregg frowned. "Let it go?"

Kris looked away, presumably to study the approaching storm. "I just put the flight school up for sale."

Gregg was silent as they turned to the larger plane and pushed it inside. "I was afraid of that."

The beep of a horn drew their attention and they looked up to see Jack drive around the corner in a beat up Suburban. He set the parking brake and swung out of the vehicle.

"Get inside, ladies. I'll help with the door."

A breathless few minutes later, Gregg slammed the passenger door and raindrops began spattering against the windshield.

"Aren't we cutting things a bit close?" Jack asked, throwing Gregg a stern look.

"Guilty as charged." Gregg suddenly looked exhausted. "You might want to think twice about this, Jack," he advised.

"Twice about what?"

"I know you're a stickler for schedules, but up to this point, there haven't been any women in your life—"

"Now, wait just one second—" Sitting in the back seat, Karen swung her fist at his shoulder just as Kayleen, sitting directly behind him, reached forward to put her hands around his throat.

"Don't believe a word he says!" Kayleen advised Jack. Then, unable to keep up the pretense, she collapsed in laughter. Karen and Gregg followed suit.

"Well, Jack," Kris said in a husky drawl, "sounds like we missed quite a trip!"

"You don't know the half of it!" Gregg turned in his seat to look back at her. "But what I want to know is why you flew that little toy all the way from California—"

"I did it as a practice run," Kris said. "A long cross-country."

Gregg squeezed his eyes shut. "I know I will regret this question." His eyes opened. "Practice run for what?"

Kris stared out the window for a moment, then looked up to hold his gaze. "I'm flying the Cub to Alaska this summer."

Watching him, Karen saw a muscle jump in Gregg's jaw.

"Say again. I thought I heard—"

"I'm flying the Piper Cub up the coast of California through Oregon and Washington until I pick up the Alaska Highway and then on to Fairbanks where I have friends with an airstrip. I plan to stay there awhile."

Gregg considered this for a moment then faced forward and slumped against the seat.

"So why make me privy to this information? Are you hoping I'll talk you out of this insanity?"

"Not at all. I'm hoping you'll give me a few pointers. You may only be the second best pilot my father ever taught to fly, but you are by far the safest. I want you to go over the route with me. Help me plot it out."

A beat of silence. "Well, if my guess is correct as to the best, the safe part is a given. How is Matt, by the way?"

"Still Matt, I would presume. I haven't seen him since Dad's funeral, and only for a moment. He did what he does best."

234

"And that would be?"

"Walk away."

Gregg muttered under his breath. "My earlier offer still holds."

A brittle laugh. "Don't think I'm not tempted!"

What earlier offer? Karen stood in the darkness and looked out at the still raging storm. Gregg and Kris made a striking pair, his darkness a foil for her blonde beauty. But neither seemed to be attracted to the other. Rather they seemed to be the very best of friends. Kris had worn Gregg down over dinner until he at least promised to go over a few sectionals with her, then they disappeared into his office.

As a trained observer, Karen had to admit that Kris was sharp, witty and charming. To say nothing of beautiful and intelligent. Karen's first impression had been that of a life-sized, animated Barbie doll—her beauty that perfect. But Kris quickly proved that her looks were only window dressing. She had a mind like a bear trap and a backbone of forged steel. As hard as she tried, Karen could not dislike this potential rival.

"You know, they've known each other for years," Anna said, coming up behind Karen. "Kris is a very special person."

"I can see that." Karen turned to look at Anna.

"At one time I might have hoped that she would be that special person for Gregg, but she gave her heart away a long time ago."

"To this 'Matt', I presume?"

"Matthew Walker, to be precise."

Karen raised her head. "Not *THE* Matt Walker?"

"Which Matt Walker would that be?" Anna smiled.

"The all-around world champion aerobatic pilot, holder of several speed and endurance records, and who knows what else. To say nothing of being the most drop-dead gorgeous man I've ever met."

"I can see he didn't make much of an impression on you," Anna said.

"It was obvious his heart was somewhere else. I was merely another pesky reporter. Now I guess I understand, not that he would have noticed me in any way other than professional. Those two are perfect for each other."

"Maybe. Maybe not. But Kris and Matt are not together, Karen. They have never been able to work out whatever differences they have."

"So how long have they been trying?"

"Almost a life time. They practically grew up together. Gregg met them after his Special Forces team rescued Matt from a downed A-10 during the first Gulf War. His first impression was that Matt was totally in love with Kris. He talked about her incessantly during his delirium."

"And then what?" Karen asked when Anna paused.

"Matt's injuries were such that he was discharged from the Air Force. Physically he mended, but mentally, he was less than whole, at least in his own mind. He let himself be totally defined by his flying. He started over and conquered another aspect of it, but still, he can't convince himself that he's good enough for Kris—that he could belong in her world."

"And how does she feel about him?" Karen asked.

"Kris would drop everything, go anywhere, at anytime, for Matt. At least at one time she would have. I think maybe this trip she is planning is an assertion that she is breaking away—becoming her own person."

"It sounds as if you approve of what she plans to do," Karen said in disbelief.

"Not entirely, but I do understand. I also have faith in her ability and her common sense. The fact that she came to Gregg underscores the latter. And she's no slouch as a pilot herself. She learned from the best, as did Matt and Gregg."

"And who would that have been?"

"Her father, Hal Holland. After his service in World War II and the Korean War, he resigned from the Air Force and started the biggest and most successful flying and aerobatic school on the West Coast. Kris has been flying from the time she was old enough to reach the controls."

"Kris and Matt are not together, Karen." Anna's words still echoed through Karen's mind as she opened her eyes the next morning. *They have never been able to work out whatever differences they have."*

"So how long have they been trying."

"Almost a life time…"

She threw back the covers and swung her feet to the floor.

Almost a lift time…

"That's not gonna happen to me," she said aloud as she reached for her clothes. *"Not in this life time…"*

Karen made her way to the pier where she could see Gregg bent over his boat. He looked up as he heard her footsteps echo along the planking.

"Good morning," she greeted.

"'Morning, yourself." He straightened to stare across the lake.

Karen studied him. She and Gregg had not talked since they returned to find Kris Holland and her Piper Cub waiting. She knew that Kris was in the hangar checking out her plane.

"Is Kris leaving this morning?" She hadn't meant to ask. It sounded as if she wanted her to go and might be interpreted as jealously.

Gregg shrugged. "Maybe. We need to check the weather again before we decide." He turned to look at Karen then, and she caught her breath at the pain she saw in his eyes.

"Gregg, what—?" Her hand went to his face, to touch his cheek.

He caught her hand and brought it to his lips. Then he drew her into his arms and tucked her head beneath his chin. She felt the tremulous sigh that shook him.

"I feel so bad for Kris—what Matt has put her through all these years. I know too well how alone she is. And the longer she is alone, the more she shuts out everyone else."

Karen drew back to look up at him. "Not unlike someone else I know."

"Yes, well, I can't see that I've gained all that much by letting someone into my life. If marrying me is all that distasteful to you—"

Karen stopped his words by putting her fingers to his lips. "I need—I want to try and explain, if you will listen."

"Is this going to be another of those *'close, very close'* explanations?"

She turned away without answering. "All my life, at least ever since I've been old enough to make decisions, they've never been simple. Someone always got hurt."

"And that someone was usually you," Gregg said flatly.

She nodded. "That's why this one has been so hard. I really can have it all this time, and I've been trying to figure out what I'm missing. Nothing can be this simple."

"I think you just lost me. As simple as what?"

"As saying yes. Except that it really is."

"Karen," Gregg's voice held a warning. "Are you trying to drive me crazy?"

She looked back at him. "I think it's too late for that. Ever since you asked me to marry you, I've been convinced you're already there."

"So only a nutcase could want you?"

"Maybe. But just in case you are in control of all your senses, and you really do want me—"

He reached for her again. "I really, *really* do want you."

She lifted her shoulders in a shrug. "The answer is yes."

His brows drew together. "Yes? Just like that."

She ran her finger along the furrow between his eyes. "What do you want? A brass band?"

He caught her chin in his hand and tipped her face up. "Not really. Just somehow I envisioned a bit of enthusiasm."

A tremor shook her. She wet her lips. "Do you have any idea how terrified I am?" she whispered. She slumped. "I was trying to put up a brave front—"

"Love!" Gregg drew her close. "Didn't I tell you that you don't have to be tough anymore—not for me!" He framed her face between his hands, kissed the tip of her nose.

She was trembling now. "I'm so afraid you'll change your mind.

Maybe that's what I'm missing. This isn't real after all—"

With a groan of frustration, Gregg tilted her head back and brought his mouth down on hers. As the kiss deepened, she reached up to twine her arms around his neck, to draw him closer.

Gregg raised his head and stared down into her face. "Tell me again that this isn't real," he growled.

Karen reached up to trace his mouth with her fingertip. "When you put it like that, it feels very real."

He reached into his pocket and drew out a small box. "I've had this in my pocket for weeks, ever since the day you left. My grandmother insisted it would bring us good luck."

Karen opened the box to reveal a dainty silver ring in the form of an unending Celtic knot. She remembered seeing it on Angela's little finger.

"Oh, Gregg, this is perfect!" she whispered.

He removed it from the box. "According to Grandmother, it is guaranteed to fit," he said as he slipped it onto the third finger of her left hand. "I thought maybe it would do until we can pick out something—"

She was shaking her head. "No. This is all I want. This and you and your family that I already love. *And forever.*"

Gregg looked into her face for a long moment. Gradually the grim lines relaxed and he drew a deep breath. His mouth curved into a smile.

"I have every intention of holding you to that promise, my love."

THE END

About the Author

Growing up in a dysfunctional home long before such terminology existed, the author found escape in books. She attributes the wholesome characters created by such authors as Emilie Loring and Grace Livingston Hill with giving direction to her life. She defined what qualities to look for and how to recognize "Mr. Right" when he came along. After a successful career as a chemist in Houston, today she lives in a private airpark in San Angelo, Texas, with her airline pilot husband of 35 years, two dogs, nine cats, lots of deer and wild turkey—and oh, yes—airplanes!

In the **HEARTland Series**, Eva O'Connor creates the characters for the books *she* wants to read. She strives to keep them wholesome enough for the daughters and granddaughters of all her friends to enjoy as well. If you enjoyed ***THE RIGHT KEY***, please look for ***PROMISES KEPT*** coming soon to lulu.com.

www.ingramcontent.com/pod-product-compliance
Lightning Source LLC
Chambersburg PA
CBHW031122030726
47496CB00002BA/650